MARCOVALDO

OTHER BOOKS BY ITALO CALVINO

Italo Calvino

MARCOVALDO

or

The seasons in the city

Translated from the Italian by
William Weaver

A Helen and Kurt Wolff Book
Harcourt Brace Jovanovich, Publishers
San Diego   New York   London

Copyright ©1963 by Giulio Einaudi editore s.p.a., Torino

English translation copyright ©1983
by Harcourt Brace Jovanovich, Inc.,
and Martin Secker & Warburg Limited

Library of Congress Cataloging in Publication Data
Calvino, Italo.
Marcovaldo, or, The seasons in the city.
Translation of: Marcovaldo, ovvero, Le stagioni in città.
"A Helen and Kurt Wolff book."
I. Title
PQ4809.A45M313   1983   853'.914   83-4372
ISBN 0-15-157081-7
ISBN 0-15-657204-4 (pbk.)

Printed in the United States of America

First American edition

A B C D E F G H I J

Author's note:

These stories take place in an industrial city of northern Italy. The first in the series were written in the early 1950s and thus are set in a very poor Italy, the Italy of neo-realistic movies. The last stories date from the mid-60s, when the illusions of an economic boom flourished.

I.C.

SPRING

1. Mushrooms in the city

The wind, coming to the city from far away, brings it unusual gifts, noticed by only a few sensitive souls, such as hay-fever victims, who sneeze at the pollen from flowers of other lands.

One day, to the narrow strip of ground flanking a city avenue came a gust of spores from God knows where; and some mushrooms germinated. Nobody noticed them except Marcovaldo, the worker who caught his tram just there every morning.

This Marcovaldo possessed an eye ill-suited to city life: billboards, traffic-lights, shop-windows, neon signs, posters, no matter how carefully devised to catch the attention, never arrested his gaze, which might have been running over the desert sands. Instead, he would never miss a leaf yellowing on a branch, a feather trapped by a roof-tile; there was no horsefly on a horse's back, no worm-hole in a plank, or fig-peel squashed on the sidewalk that Marcovaldo didn't remark and ponder over, discovering the changes of season, the yearnings of his heart, and the woes of his existence.

Thus, one morning, as he was waiting for the tram that would take him to Sbav and Co., where he was employed as an unskilled laborer, he noticed something unusual near the stop, in the sterile, encrusted strip of earth beneath the

1

avenue's line of trees; at certain points, near the tree trunks, some bumps seemed to rise and, here and there, they had opened, allowing roundish subterranean bodies to peep out.

Bending to tie his shoes, he took a better look: they were mushrooms, real mushrooms, sprouting right in the heart of the city! To Marcovaldo the gray and wretched world surrounding him seemed suddenly generous with hidden riches; something could still be expected of life, beyond the hourly wage of his stipulated salary, with inflation index, family grant, and cost-of-living allowance.

On the job he was more absent-minded than usual; he kept thinking that while he was there unloading cases and boxes, in the darkness of the earth the slow, silent mushrooms, known only to him, were ripening their porous flesh, were assimilating underground humors, breaking the crust of clods. "One night's rain would be enough," he said to himself, "then they would be ready to pick." And he couldn't wait to share his discovery with his wife and his six children.

"I'm telling you!" he announced during their scant supper. "In a week's time we'll be eating mushrooms! A great fry! That's a promise!"

And to the smaller children, who did not know what mushrooms were, he explained ecstatically the beauty of the numerous species, the delicacy of their flavor, the way they should be cooked; and so he also drew into the discussion his wife, Domitilla, who until then had appeared rather incredulous and abstracted.

"Where are these mushrooms?" the children asked. "Tell us where they grow!"

At this question Marcovaldo's enthusiasm was curbed by a suspicious thought: Now if I tell them the place, they'll go and hunt for them with the usual gang of kids, word will spread through the neighborhood, and the mushrooms will end up in somebody else's pan! And so that discovery, which had promptly filled his heart with universal love, now made him wildly possessive, surrounded him with jealous and distrusting fear.

"I know where the mushrooms are, and I'm the only one who knows," he said to his children, "and God help you if you breathe a word to anybody."

The next morning, as he approached the tram stop, Marcovaldo was filled with apprehension. He bent to look at the ground and, to his relief, saw that the mushrooms had grown a little, but not much, and were still almost completely hidden by the earth.

He was bent in this position when he realized there was someone behind him. He straightened up at once and tried to act indifferent. It was the street-cleaner, leaning on his broom and looking at him.

This street-cleaner, whose jurisdiction included the place where the mushrooms grew, was a lanky youth with eyeglasses. His name was Amadigi, and Marcovaldo had long harbored a dislike of him, perhaps because of those eyeglasses that examined the pavement of the streets, seeking any trace of nature, to be eradicated by his broom.

It was Saturday; and Marcovaldo spent his free half-day circling the bed of dirt with an absent air, keeping an eye on the street-cleaner in the distance and on the mushrooms, and calculating how much time they needed to ripen.

That night it rained: like peasants who, after months of drought, wake up and leap with joy at the sound of the first drops, so Marcovaldo, alone in all the city, sat up in bed and called to his family: "It's raining! It's raining!" and breathed in the smell of moistened dust and fresh mold that came from outside.

At dawn – it was Sunday – with the children and a borrowed basket, he ran immediately to the patch. There were the mushrooms, erect on their stems, their caps high over the still-soaked earth. "Hurrah!" – and they fell to gathering them.

"Papà! Look how many that man over there has found," Michelino said, and his father, raising his eyes, saw Amadigi standing beside them, also with a basket full of mushrooms under his arm.

"Ah, you're gathering them, too?" the street-cleaner said. "Then they're edible? I picked a few, but I wasn't sure . . . Farther down the avenue some others have sprouted, even bigger ones . . . Well, now that I know, I'll tell my relatives; they're down there arguing whether it's a good idea to pick them or not . . ." And he walked off in a hurry.

Marcovaldo was speechless: even bigger mushrooms, which he hadn't noticed, an unhoped-for harvest, being taken from him like this, before his very eyes. For a moment he was almost frozen with anger, fury, then – as sometimes happens – the collapse of individual passion led to a generous impulse. At that hour, many people were waiting for the tram, umbrellas over their arms, because the weather was still damp and uncertain. "Hey, you! Do you want to eat fried mushrooms tonight?" Marcovaldo shouted to the crowd of people at the stop. "Mushrooms are growing here by the street! Come along! There's plenty for all!" And he walked off after Amadigi, with a string of people behind him.

They all found plenty of mushrooms, and lacking baskets, they used their open umbrellas. Somebody said: "It would be nice to have a big feast, all of us together!" But, instead, each took his own share and went home.

They saw one another again soon, however; that very evening, in fact, in the same ward of the hospital, after the stomach-pump had saved them all from poisoning. It was not serious, because the number of mushrooms eaten by each person was quite small.

Marcovaldo and Amadigi had adjacent beds; they glared at each other.

SUMMER

2. Park-bench vacation

On his way to work each morning, Marcovaldo walked beneath the green foliage of a square with trees, a bit of public garden, isolated in the junction of four streets. He raised his eyes among the boughs of the horse-chestnuts, where they were at their thickest and allowed yellow rays only to glint in the shade transparent with sap; and he listened to the racket of the sparrows, tone-deaf, invisible on the branches. To him they seemed nightingales, and he said to himself: "Oh, if I could wake just once at the twitter of birds and not at the sound of the alarm and the crying of little Paolino and the yelling of my wife, Domitilla!" or else: "Oh, if I could sleep here, alone, in the midst of this cool green shade and not in my cramped, hot room; here amid the silence, not amid the snoring and sleep-talking of my whole family and the racing of trams down below in the street; here in the natural darkness of the night, not in the artificial darkness of closed blinds, streaked by the glare of headlights; oh, if I could see leaves and sky on opening my eyes!" With these thoughts every day Marcovaldo began his eight daily hours – plus overtime – as an unskilled laborer.

In one corner of the square, under a dome of horse-chestnuts, there was a remote, half-hidden bench. And Marcovaldo had picked it as his own. On those summer nights, in the room where five of them slept, when he

5

couldn't get to sleep, he would dream of the bench as a vagabond dreams of a bed in a palace. One night, quietly, while his wife snored and the children kicked in their sleep, he got out of bed, dressed, tucked his pillow under his arm, left the house and went to the square.

There it was cool, peaceful. He was already savoring the contact of those planks, whose wood – he knew – was soft and cozy, preferable in every respect to the flattened mattress of his bed; he would look for a moment at the stars, then close his eyes in a sleep that would compensate him for all the insults of the day.

Cool and peace he found, but not the empty bench. A couple of lovers were sitting there, looking into each other's eyes. Discreetly, Marcovaldo withdrew. "It's late," he thought, "they surely won't spend the whole night outdoors! They'll come to an end of their billing and cooing."

But the two were not billing or cooing: they were quarreling. And when lovers start to quarrel there's no telling how long it will go on.

He was saying: "Why don't you admit that when you said what you said you knew you were going to hurt me and not make me happy the way you were pretending you thought?"

Marcovaldo realized it was going to last quite a while.

"No, I will not admit it," she answered, as Marcovaldo had already expected.

"Why won't you admit it?"

"I'll never admit it."

Damn, Marcovaldo thought. His pillow clutched under his arm, he went for a stroll. He went and looked at the moon, which was full, big above trees and roofs. He came back towards the bench, giving it a fairly wide berth out of fear of disturbing them, but actually hoping to irritate them a little and persuade them to go away. But they were too caught up in the argument to notice him.

"You admit it then?"

"No, no, I don't admit it in the least!"

"But what if you did admit it?"

"Even if I did admit something, I wouldn't admit what you want me to admit!"

Marcovaldo went back to look at the moon, then he went to look at a traffic-light, a bit farther on. The light flashed yellow, yellow, yellow, constantly blinking on and off. Marcovaldo compared the moon with the traffic-light. The moon with her mysterious pallor, also yellow, but also green, in its depths, and even blue; the traffic-light with its common little yellow. And the moon, all calm, casting her light without haste, streaked now and then by fine wisps of clouds, which she majestically allowed to fall around her shoulders; and the traffic-light meanwhile, always there, on and off, on and off, throbbing with a false vitality, but actually weary and enslaved.

He went back to see if the girl had admitted anything. Not on your life: no admission from her. In fact, she wasn't now the one who refused to admit; he was. The situation had changed completely, and it was she who kept saying to him: "Then you admit it?", and he kept saying no. A half hour went by like this. In the end, he admitted, or she did; anyway, Marcovaldo saw them get up and walk off, hand in hand.

He ran to the bench, flung himself on it; but meanwhile, in his waiting, he had lost some of his propensity to feel the sweetness he had been expecting to find there, and his bed at home, as he now remembered it, wasn't as hard as it had been. But these were minor points; his determination to enjoy the night in the open air remained firm. He stuck his face in the pillow and prepared for sleep, the kind of sleep to which he had long become unaccustomed.

Now he had found the most comfortable position. He wouldn't have shifted a fraction of an inch for anything in the world. Too bad, though, that when he lay like this, his gaze didn't fall on a prospect of trees and sky alone, so that in sleep his eyes would close on a view of absolute natural serenity. Before him, foreshortened, a tree was followed by the sword of a general from the height of his monument, then another tree, a notice-board, a third tree, and then, a bit farther, that false, flashing moon, the traffic-light, still ticking off its yellow, yellow, yellow.

It must be said that Marcovaldo's nervous system had been in such poor shape lately that even when he was dead tired a trifle sufficed to keep him awake; he had only to think something was annoying him, and sleep was out of the question. And now he was annoyed by that traffic-light blinking on and off. It was there in the distance, a yellow eye, winking, alone: it was nothing to bother about. But Marcovaldo must have been suffering from nervous exhaustion: he stared at that blinking and repeated to himself: "How I would sleep if that thing wasn't there! How I would sleep!" He closed his eyes and seemed to feel, under his eyelids, that silly yellow blinking; he screwed his eyes shut and he could see dozens of traffic-lights; he reopened his eyes, it was the same thing all over again.

He got up. He had to put some screen between himself and the traffic-light. He went as far as the general's monument and looked around. At the foot of the monument there was a laurel wreath, nice and thick, but now dry and coming apart, standing on props, with a broad, faded ribbon: "*The 15th Lancers on the Anniversary of The Glorious Victory.*" Marcovaldo climbed up on the pedestal, raised the wreath, and hung it on the general's sabre.

Tornaquinci, the night watchman, making his rounds, crossed the square on his bicycle; Marcovaldo hid behind the statue. Tornaquinci saw the shadow of the monument move on the ground: he stopped, filled with suspicion. He studied that wreath on the sabre: he realized something was out of place, but didn't know quite what. He aimed the beam of his flashlight up there; he read: "*The 15th Lancers on the Anniversary of The Glorious Victory.*" He nodded approvingly and went away.

To give him time to go off, Marcovaldo made another turn around the square. In a nearby street, a team of workmen was repairing a switch of the tram-track. At night, in the deserted streets, those little groups of men huddling in the glow of the welding torches, their voices ringing, then dying immediately, have a secret look, as of people preparing things the inhabitants of the daytime must never know. Marcovaldo approached, stood looking at the flame, the workmen's movements, with a somewhat embarrassed attention, his eyes growing smaller and smaller with sleepiness. He hunted for a cigarette in his pocket, to keep himself awake; but he had no matches. "Who'll give me a light?" he asked the workmen. "With this?" the man with the torch said, spraying a flurry of sparks.

Another workman stood up, handed him a lighted cigarette. "Do you work nights, too?"

"No, I work days," Marcovaldo said.

"Then what are you doing up at this time of night? We're about to quit."

He went back to the bench. He stretched out. Now the traffic-light was hidden from his eyes; he could fall asleep, at last.

He hadn't noticed the noise, before. Now, that buzz, like a grim, inhaling breath and an endless scraping and also a scratching, filled his ears completely. There is no sound more heart-rending than that of a welding torch, a kind of muffled scream. Without moving, huddled as he was on the bench, his face against the crumpled pillow, Marcovaldo could find no escape, and the noise continued to conjure up the scene illuminated by the gray flame scattering golden sparks all around, the men hunkered on the ground, smoked-glass vizors over their faces, the torch grasped in the hand shaken by a rapid tremor, the halo of shadow around the tool cart, at the tall trellis-like apparatus that reached the wires. He opened his eyes, turned on the bench, looked at the stars among the boughs. The insensitive sparrows continued sleeping up there among the leaves.

To fall asleep like a bird, to have a wing you could stick

your head under, a world of branches suspended above the earthly world, barely glimpsed down below, muffled and remote. Once you begin rejecting your present state, there is no knowing where you can arrive. Now Marcovaldo, in order to sleep, needed something; but he himself didn't know quite what; at this point not even a genuine silence would have been enough. He had to have a basis of sound, softer than silence, a faint wind passing through the thick undergrowth of a forest, a murmur of water bubbling up and disappearing in a meadow.

He had an idea and he rose to his feet. It wasn't exactly an idea, because half-dazed by the sleepiness that filled him, he couldn't form any thought properly; but it was like a re-collection that somewhere around there was something connected with the idea of water, with its loquacious and subdued flow.

In fact, there was a fountain, nearby, a distinguished work of sculpture and hydraulics, with nymphs, fauns, river gods, who enlaced jets, cascades, a play of water. Only it was dry: at night, in summer, since the aqueduct was functioning less, they turned it off. Marcovaldo wandered around for a little while like a sleep-walker; more by instinct than by reason he knew that a tub must have a tap. A man who has a good eye can find what he is looking for even with his eyes closed. He turned on the tap: from the conch-shells, from the beards, from the nostrils of the horses, great jets rose, the feigned caverns were cloaked in glistening mantles, and all this water resounded like the organ of a choir loft in the great empty square, with all the rustling and turbulence that water can create. The night watchman, Tornaquinci, was coming along again on his coal-black bicycle, thrusting his tickets under doorways, when he suddenly saw the whole fountain explode before his eyes like a liquid firework. He nearly fell off his seat.

Trying to open his eyes as little as possible, to retain that shred of sleep he felt he had grasped, Marcovaldo ran and flung himself again on the bench. There, now it was as if he lay on the bank of a stream, with the woods above him; he slept.

He dreamed of a dinner, the dish was covered as if to keep the pasta warm. He uncovered it and there was a dead mouse, which stank. He looked into his wife's plate: another dead mouse. Before his children, more mice, smaller, but also rotting. He uncovered the tureen and found a cat, belly in the air; and the stink woke him.

Not far away there was the garbage truck that passes at night to empty the garbage cans. He could make out in the dim glow from the headlights, the crane, cackling and jerking, the shadows of men standing on the top of the mountain of refuse, their hands guiding the receptacle attached to the pulley, emptying it into the truck, pounding it with blows of their shovels, their voices grim and jerky like the movement of the crane: "Higher . . . let it go . . . to hell with you . . .," with metallic clashes like opaque gongs, and then the engine picking up, slowly, only to stop a bit farther on, as the maneuver began all over again.

But by now Marcovaldo's sleep had reached a zone where sounds no longer arrived, and these, even so graceless and rasping, came as if muffled in a soft halo, perhaps because of the very consistency of the garbage packed into the trucks. It was the stink that kept him awake, the stink sharpened by an unbearable idea of stink, whereby even the sounds, those dampened and remote sounds, and the image, outlined against the light, of the truck with the crane didn't reach his mind as sound and sight but only as stink. And Marcovaldo was delirious, vainly pursuing with his nostrils' imagination the fragrance of a rose arbor.

The night watchman, Tornaquinci, felt sweat bathe his forehead as he glimpsed a human form running on all fours along a flower-bed, then saw it angrily rip up some buttercups, then disappear. But he thought it must have been either a dog, the responsibility of dog-catchers, or a hallucination, the responsibility of the alienist, or a

were-wolf, the responsibility of God knows who but prefer-
ably not him; and he turned the corner.

Meanwhile, having gone back to his sleeping place,
Marcovaldo pressed the bedraggled clump of buttercups to
his nose, trying to fill his sense of smell to the brim with
their perfume: but he could press very little from those
almost odorless flowers. Still the fragrance of dew, of earth,
and of trampled grass was already a great balm. He dispelled
the obsession of garbage and slept. It was dawn.

His waking was a sudden explosion of sun-filled sky
above his head, a sun that virtually obliterated the leaves,
then restored them gradually to his half-blinded sight. But
Marcovaldo could not stay because a shiver had made him
jump up: the spatter of a hydrant, which the city gardeners
use for watering the flowerbeds, made cold streams trickle
down his clothes. And all around there were trams clamor-
ing, trucks going to market, hand-carts, pickups, workers
on motorbikes rushing to factories, and the blinds being
rolled up at house windows whose panes were glittering.
His mouth and eyes sticky, his back stiff and one hip
bruised, bewildered, Marcovaldo rushed to work.

AUTUMN

3. The municipal pigeon

The routes birds follow, as they migrate southwards or northwards, in autumn or in spring, rarely cross the city. Their flights cleave the heavens high above the striped humps of fields and along the edge of woods; at one point they seem to follow the curving line of a river or the furrow of a valley; at another, the invisible paths of the wind. But they sheer off as soon as the range of a city's rooftops looms up before them.

And yet, once, a flight of autumn woodcock appeared in a street's slice of sky. And the only person to notice was Marcovaldo, who always walked with his nose in the air. He was on a little tricycle-truck, and seeing the birds he pedaled harder, as if he were chasing them, in the grip of a hunter's fantasy, though the only gun he had ever held was an army rifle.

And as he proceeded, his eyes on the flying birds, he found himself at an intersection, the light red, in the midst of the automobiles; and he came within a hair's breadth of being run over. As a traffic cop, his face purple, wrote name and address in a notebook, Marcovaldo sought again with his eyes those wings in the sky; but they had vanished.

At work, his fine brought him harsh reproaches.

"Can't you even get traffic-lights straight?" his foreman,

13

Signor Viligelmo, shouted at him. "What were you looking
at anyway, knuckle-head?"

"I was looking at a flight of woodcock . . ." he said.

"What?" Signor Viligelmo was an old man; his eyes
glistened. And Marcovaldo told him the story.

"Saturday I'm going out with dog and gun!" the foreman
said, full of vigor, now forgetting his outburst. "The
migration's begun, up in the hills. Those birds were certainly
scared off by the hunters up there, and they flew over the
city . . ."

All that day Marcovaldo's brain ground and ground, like
a mill. "Saturday, if the hills are full of hunters, as is quite
likely, God knows how many woodcock will fly over the
city. If I handle it right, Sunday I'll eat roast woodcock."

The building where Marcovaldo lived had a flat roof,
with wires strung for drying laundry. Marcovaldo climbed
up there with three of his children, carrying a can of birdlime, a brush, and a sack of corn. While the children scattered
kernels of corn everywhere, he spread birdlime on the
parapets, the wires, the frames of the chimneypots. He put
so much on that Filippetto, while he was playing, almost
got stuck fast.

That night Marcovaldo dreamed of the roof dotted with
fluttering, trapped woodcock. His wife, Domitilla, more
greedy and lazy, dreamed of ducks already roasted, lying on
the chimneys. His daughter Isolina, romantic, dreamed of
humming-birds to decorate her hat. Michelino dreamed of
finding a stork up there.

The next day, every hour one of the children went up to
inspect the roof: he would just peek out from the trap-door
so, if they were about to alight, they wouldn't be scared;
then he would come down and report. The reports were not
good. But then, towards noon, Pietruccio came back,
shouting: "They're here! Papà! Come and see!"

Marcovaldo went up with a sack. Trapped in the birdlime
there was a poor pigeon, one of those gray urban doves,

used to the crowds and racket of the squares. Fluttering around, other pigeons contemplated him sadly, as he tried to unstick his wings from the mess on which he had unwisely lighted.

Marcovaldo and his family were sucking the little bones of that thin and stringy pigeon, which had been roasted, when they heard a knocking at the door.

It was the landlady's maid. "The Signora wants you! Come at once!"

Very concerned, because he was six months behind with the rent and feared eviction, Marcovaldo went to the Signora's apartment, on the main floor. As he entered the living room, he saw that there was already a visitor: the purple-faced cop.

"Come in, Marcovaldo," the Signora said. "I am informed that on our roof someone is trapping the city's pigeons. Do you know anything about it?"

Marcovaldo felt himself freeze.

"Signora! Signora!" a woman's voice cried at that moment.

"What is it, Guendalina?"

The laundress came in. "I went up to hang out the laundry, and all the wash is stuck to the lines. I pulled on it, to get it loose, but it tore. Everything's ruined. What can it be?"

Marcovaldo rubbed his hand over his stomach, as if his digestion were giving him trouble.

WINTER

4. The city lost in the snow

That morning the silence woke him. Marcovaldo pulled himself out of bed with the sensation there was something strange in the air. He couldn't figure out what time it was, the light between the slats of the blinds was different from all other hours of day and night. He opened the window: the city was gone; it had been replaced by a white sheet of paper. Narrowing his eyes, he could make out, in the whiteness, some almost-erased lines, which corresponded to those of the familiar view: the windows and the roofs and the lamp-posts all around, but they were lost under all the snow that had settled over them during the night.

"Snow!" Marcovaldo cried to his wife; that is, he meant to cry, but his voice came out muffled. As it had fallen on lines and colors and views, the snow had fallen on noises, or rather on the very possibility of making noise; sounds, in a padded space, did not vibrate.

He went to work on foot; the trams were blocked by the snow. Along the street, making his own path, he felt free as he had never felt before. In the city all differences between sidewalk and street had vanished; vehicles could not pass, and Marcovaldo, even if he sank up to his thighs at every step and felt the snow get inside his socks, had become master, free to walk in the middle of the street, to trample on flower-beds, to cross outside the prescribed lines, to proceed in a zig-zag.

Streets and avenues stretched out, endless and deserted, like blanched chasms between mountainous cliffs. There was no telling whether the city hidden under that mantle was still the same or whether, in the night, another had taken its place. Who could say if under those white mounds there were still gasoline pumps, news-stands, tram stops, or if there were only sack upon sack of snow? As he walked along, Marcovaldo dreamed of getting lost in a different city: instead, his footsteps were taking him straight to his everyday place of work, the usual shipping department, and, once he had crossed the threshold, the worker was amazed at finding himself among those walls, the same as ever, as if the change that had cancelled the outside world had spared only his firm.

There, waiting for him, was a shovel, taller than he was. The department foreman, Signor Viligelmo, handing it to him, said: "Shoveling the snow off the sidewalk in front of the building is up to us. To you, that is." Marcovaldo took the shovel and went outside again.

Shoveling snow is no game, especially on an empty stomach; but Marcovaldo felt the snow was a friend, an element that erased the cage of walls which imprisoned his life. And he set to work with a will, sending great shovelfuls of snow flying from the sidewalk to the center of the street.

The jobless Sigismondo was also filled with gratitude for the snow, because having enrolled in the ranks of the municipal snow-shovelers that morning, he now had before him a few days of guaranteed employment. But this feeling, instead of inspiring in him vague fantasies like Marcovaldo's, led him to quite specific calculations, to determine how many cubic feet of snow had to be shoveled to clear so many square feet. In other words, he aimed at impressing the captain of his team; and thus – his secret ambition – at getting ahead in the world.

Now Sigismondo turned, and what did he see? The stretch of road he had just cleared was being covered again with snow, by the helter-skelter shoveling of a character panting there on the sidewalk. Sigismondo almost had a fit. He ran and confronted the other man, thrusting at the stranger's chest his shovel piled high with snow. "Hey, you! Are you the one who's been throwing that snow there?"

"Eh? What?" Marcovaldo started, but admitted, "Ah, maybe I am."

"Well, either you take it right back with your shovel, or I'll make you eat it, down to the last flake."

"But I have to clear the sidewalk."

"And I have to clear the street. So?"

"Where'll I put it?"

"Do you work for the City?"

"No. For Sbav and Co."

Sigismondo taught him how to pile up the snow along the edge of the sidewalk, and Marcovaldo cleared his whole stretch. Content, sticking their shovels into the snow, the two men stood and contemplated their achievement.

"Got a butt?" Sigismondo asked.

They were lighting half a cigarette apiece, when a snow-plow came along the street, raising two big white waves that fell at either side. Every sound that morning was a mere rustle: by the time the men raised their heads, the whole section they had shoveled was again covered with snow. "What happened? Has it started snowing again?" And they looked up at the sky. The machine, spinning its huge brushes, was already turning at the corner.

Marcovaldo learned to pile the snow into a compact little wall. If he went on making little walls like that, he could build some streets for himself alone; only he would know where those streets led, and everybody else would be lost there. He could remake the city, pile up mountains high as houses, which no one would be able to tell from real houses. But perhaps by now all the houses had turned to snow, inside and out; a whole city of snow with monuments and spires and trees, a city that could be unmade by shovel and remade in a different way.

On the edge of the sidewalk at a certain point there was a considerable heap of snow. Marcovaldo was about to level it to the height of his little walls when he realized it was an automobile: the de-luxe car of Commendatore Alboino, chairman of the board, all covered with snow. Since the difference between an automobile and a pile of snow was so slight, Marcovaldo began creating the form of an automobile with his shovel. It came out well: you really couldn't tell which of the two was real. To put the final touches on his work Marcovaldo used some rubbish that had turned up in his shovel: a rusted tin served to model the shape of a headlight; an old tap gave the door its handle.

A great bowing and scraping of doormen, attendants and flunkies, and the chairman, Commendatore Alboino, came out of the main entrance. Short-sighted and efficient, he strode straight to his car, grasped the protruding tap, pulled it down, bowed his head, and stepped into the pile of snow up to his neck.

Marcovaldo had already turned the corner and was shoveling in the courtyard.

The boys in the yard had made a snow man. "He needs a nose!" one of them said. "What'll we use? A carrot!" And they ran to their various kitchens to hunt among the vegetables.

Marcovaldo contemplated the snow man. "There, under the snow you can't tell what is snow and what is only covered. Except in one case: man; because it's obvious I am I and not this man here."

Absorbed in his meditations, he didn't hear two men shouting from the rooftop: "Hey, mister, get out of the way!" They were the men responsible for pushing the snow off the roof-tiles. And all of a sudden, about three hundred-weight of snow fell right on top of him.

The children returned with their looted carrots. "Oh, they've made another snow man!" In the courtyard there were two identical dummies, side by side.

"We'll give them each a nose!" And they thrust carrots into the heads of the two snow men.

More dead than alive, Marcovaldo, through the sheath in which he was buried and frozen, felt some nourishment reach him. And he chewed on it.

"Hey, look! The carrot's gone!" The children were very frightened.

The bravest of the boys didn't lose heart. He had a spare nose: a pepper, and he stuck it into the snow man. The snow man ate that, too.

Then they tried giving him a nose made out of coal, a big lump. Marcovaldo spat it out with all his might. "Help! He's alive! He's alive!" The children ran away.

In a corner of the courtyard there was a grille from which a cloud of warmth emerged. With the heavy tread of a snow man, Marcovaldo went and stood there. The snow melted over him, trickled in rivulets down his clothes: a Marcovaldo reappeared, all swollen and stuffed up with a cold.

He took the shovel, mostly to warm himself, and began to work in the courtyard. There was a sneeze blocked at the top of his nose, all ready and waiting, but refusing to make up its mind and burst forth. Marcovaldo shoveled, his eyes half-closed, and the sneeze remained nested in the top of his nose. All of a sudden: the "Aaaaaah . . ." was almost a roar, and the "choo!" was louder than the explosion of a mine. The blast flung Marcovaldo against the wall.

Blast, indeed: that sneeze had caused a genuine tornado. All the snow in the courtyard rose and whirled in a blizzard, drawn upwards, pulverized in the sky.

When Marcovaldo reopened his eyes, after being stunned, the courtyard was completely cleared, with not even one flake of snow. And to his gaze there appeared the familiar courtyard, the gray walls, the boxes from the warehouse, the things of every day, sharp and hostile.

SPRING

5. The wasp treatment

Winter departed and left rheumatic aches behind. A faint noonday sun came to cheer the days, and Marcovaldo would spend a few hours watching the leaves sprout, as he sat on a bench, waiting to go back to work. Near him a little old man would come and sit, hunched in his overcoat, all patches: he was a certain Signor Rizieri, retired, all alone in the world, and also a regular visitor of sunny park benches. From time to time this Signor Rizieri would jerk and cry – "Ow!" – and hunch even deeper into his coat. He was a mass of rheumatism, arthritis, lumbago, collected during the damp, cold winter, which continued to pursue him for the rest of the year. To console him, Marcovaldo would explain the various stages of his own rheumatic pains, as well as those of his wife and of his oldest daughter, Isolina, who, poor thing, was turning out to be rather delicate.

Every day Marcovaldo carried his lunch wrapped in newspaper; seated on the bench he would unwrap it and give the crumpled piece of newspaper to Signor Rizieri, who would hold out his hand impatiently, saying: "Let's see what the news is." He always read it with the same interest, even if it was two years old.

And so one day he came upon an article about a method of curing rheumatism with bee venom.

"They must mean honey," Marcovaldo said, always inclined to be optimistic.

"No," Rizieri said, "venom, it says here: the poison in the sting." And he read a few passages aloud. The two of them discussed bees at length, their virtues, attributes, and also the possible cost of this treatment.

After that, as he walked along the avenues, Marcovaldo pricked up his ears at every buzz, his gaze followed every insect that flew around him. And so, observing the circling of a wasp with a big black-and-yellow-striped belly, he saw it burrow into the hollow of a tree, where other wasps then came out: a thrumming, a bustle that announced the presence of a whole wasp-nest inside the trunk. Marcovaldo promptly began his hunt. He had a glass jar, in the bottom of which there was still a thick layer of jam. He placed it, open, near the tree. Soon a wasp buzzed around it, then went inside, attracted by the sugary smell. Marcovaldo was quick to cover the jar with a paper lid.

And the moment he saw Signor Rizieri, he could say to him: "Come, I'll give you the injection!", showing him the jar with the infuriated wasp trapped inside.

The old man hesitated, but Marcovaldo refused to postpone the experiment for any reason, and insisted on performing it right there, on their bench: the patient didn't even have to undress. With a mixture of fear and hope, Signor Rizieri raised the hem of his overcoat, his jacket, his shirt; and opening a space through his tattered undershirts, he uncovered a part of his loins where he ached. Marcovaldo stuck the top of the jar there and slipped away the paper that was acting as a lid. At first nothing happened; the wasp didn't move. Had he gone to sleep? To waken him, Marcovaldo gave the bottom of the jar a whack. That whack was just what was needed: the insect darted forward and jabbed his sting into Signor Rizieri's loins. The old man let out a yell, jumped to his feet, and began walking like a soldier on parade, rubbing the stung part and emitting a string of confused curses.

Marcovaldo was all content; the old man had never been so erect, so martial. But a policeman had stopped nearby, and was staring wide-eyed; Marcovaldo took Rizieri by the arm and went off, whistling.

He came home with another wasp in the jar. To convince his wife to allow the sting was no easy matter, but in the end he succeeded. For a while, at least Domitilla complained only of the wasp sting.

Marcovaldo started catching wasps full tilt. He gave Isolina an injection, and Domitilla a second one, because only systematic treatment could bring about an improvement. Then he decided to have a shot himself. The children, you know how they are, were saying: "Me, too; me, too," but Marcovaldo preferred to equip them with jars and set them to catching more wasps, to supply the daily requirements.

Signor Rizieri came to Marcovaldo's house looking for him; he had another old man with him, Cavalier Ulrico, who dragged one leg and wanted to start the treatment at once.

Word spread; Marcovaldo now had an assembly-line set up: he always kept half a dozen wasps in stock, each in its glass jar, lined up on a shelf. He applied the jar to the patient's behind as if it were a syringe, he pulled away the paper lid, and when the wasp had stung, he rubbed the place with alcohol-soaked cotton, with the nonchalant hand of an experienced physician. His house consisted of a single room, in which the whole family slept; they divided it with a makeshift screen, waiting-room on one side, doctor's office on the other. In the waiting-room Marcovaldo's wife received the clients and collected the fees. The children took the empty jars and ran off towards the wasps' nest for refills. Sometimes a wasp would sting them, but they hardly cried any more, because they knew it was good for their health.

That year rheumatic aches and pains twisted among the population like the tentacles of an octopus; Marcovaldo's cure acquired great renown; and on Saturday afternoon he saw his poor garret invaded by a little throng of suffering men and women, pressing a hand to their back or hip, some with the tattered aspect of beggars, others looking like well-off people, drawn by the novelty of this treatment.

"Hurry," Marcovaldo said to his three boys, "take the jars, go and catch as many wasps as you can." The boys went off.

It was a sunny day, many wasps were buzzing along the avenue. The boys usually hunted them at a certain distance from the tree where their nest was, trying to catch isolated insects. But that day, Michelino, to save time and catch more, began hunting right at the entrance to the nest. "This is the way to do it," he said to his brothers, and he tried to catch a wasp by putting the jar over it the moment it landed. But, every time, that wasp flew away and came back to light closer and and closer to the nest. Now it was at the very edge of the hollow in the trunk, and Michelino was about to lower the jar on it, when he felt two other big wasps fling themselves on him as if they wanted to sting him on the head. He shielded himself, but he felt the prick of the stings and, crying out in pain, he dropped the jar. Immediately, dismay at what he had done erased his pain: the jar had fallen into the mouth of the nest. No further buzzing was heard, no more wasps came out; Michelino, without even the strength to yell, took a step backwards. Then from the nest a thick, black cloud burst out, with a deafening hum: all the wasps were advancing at once in an enraged swarm!

His brothers heard Michelino let out a scream as he began running as he had never run in his life. He seemed steam-driven, as that cloud he trailed after him seemed the smoke from a chimney.

Where does a child run when he is being chased? He runs home! And that's what Michelino did.

The passers-by didn't have time to realize what that sight was, something between a cloud and a human being, darting along the streets with a roar mixed with a loud buzz.

Marcovaldo was saying to his patients: "Just one moment,

the wasps will soon be here," when the door opened and the swarm invaded the room. They didn't even see Michelino, who went to stick his head in a basin of water: the whole room was full of wasps and the patients flapped their arms in the futile effort to drive them away, and the rheumatics performed wonders of agility and the benumbed limbs were released in furious movements.

The fire department came, and then the Red Cross. Lying on his cot in the hospital, swollen beyond recognition by the stings, Marcovaldo didn't dare react to the curses that were hurled at him from the other cots of the ward by his patients.

SUMMER

6. A Saturday of sun, sand, and sleep

"For your rheumatism," the Public Health doctor had said, "this summer you should take some sand treatments." And so, one Saturday afternoon, Marcovaldo was exploring the banks of the river, looking for a place where the sand was dry and in the sun. But wherever there was sand, the river was only a clank of rusty chains; dredgers and derricks were at work: machines as old as dinosaurs digging into the river and emptying giant spoonfuls of sand into the contractors' dump-trucks parked there among the willows. The conveyor line of buckets rose erect and descended overturned, and the cranes lifted on their long neck a pelican-like gullet spilling gobbets of the black muck of the river-bed. Marcovaldo bent to touch the sand, crushed it in his palm; it was wet, a mush, a mire: even where the sun had formed a dry and crumbling crust, an inch below it was still damp.

Marcovaldo's children, whom their father had brought along hoping to put them to work covering him with sand, couldn't contain their desire to go swimming. "Papà, papà, we're going to dive! We're going to swim in the river!"

"Are you crazy? There's a sign: 'All swimming forbidden.' You'd drown, you'd sink like stones!" And he explained that, where the river-bed has been excavated by dredgers, there remain hollow funnels that suck the stream down in eddies or whirlpools.

26

"Whirlpools! Show us the whirlpools!" For the children, the word had a jolly sound.

"You can't see one; it grabs you by the foot, while you're swimming, and drags you down."

"What about that? Why doesn't it go down? Is it a fish?"

"No, it's a dead cat," Marcovaldo explained. "It floats because its belly is full of water."

"Does the whirlpool catch the cat by its tail?" Michelino asked.

The slope of the grassy bank, at a certain point, opened out in a rather flat clearing where a big sifter had been set up. Two men were sifting a pile of sand, using shovels, and with the same shovels they then loaded it on a black, shallow barge, a kind of raft, which floated there, tied to a willow. The two bearded men worked under the fierce sun wearing hats and jackets, but torn and moldy, and trousers ending in shreds at the knee, leaving legs and feet bare.

In that sand, left to dry for days and days, fine, cleansed of impurities, pale as the sand at the seaside, Marcovaldo recognized what was needed for him. But he had discovered it too late: they were already loading it onto that barge, to take it away . . .

No, not yet: the sandmen, having completed their loading, broke out a flask of wine, and after passing it back and forth a couple of times drinking in gulps, they lay down in the shade of the willows while the hour of greatest heat passed.

"As long as they are sleeping, I can lie down in their sand and have a sand pack!" Marcovaldo thought, and he ordered the children, in a low voice: "Quick, help me!"

He jumped on the barge, took off shirt, trousers and shoes, and burrowed into the sand. "Cover me! With the shovel!" he said to the children. "No, not my head; I need that to breathe with. It has to stay outside. All the rest!"

For the children it was like building a sand-castle. "Shall we make sand-pies? No, a castle with ramparts! No, no, it makes a nice track for marbles!"

"Go away now!" Marcovaldo huffed, from beneath his sarcophagus of sand. "No, first put a paper hat over my forehead and eyes. And then jump ashore and go play a bit farther off, otherwise the men will wake up and drive me away."

"We can tow you down the river, pulling the barge-rope from the shore," Filippetto suggested, when he had already half-untied the mooring.

Marcovaldo, immobilized, twisted his mouth and eyes to scold them. "If you don't go away right now, if you make me get up from here, I'll beat you with the shovel!" The kids ran off.

The sun blazed, the sand burned, and Marcovaldo, dripping sweat under his paper hat, felt, as he lay there motionless, enduring the baking, the sense of satisfaction produced by painful treatments or nasty medicines, when you think: "The worse it is, the more good it's doing me."

He dozed off, rocked by the slight current that first tautened the mooring a little, then loosened it. In this pulling to and fro, the knot, which Filippetto had already half undone, became undone altogether. And the barge laden with sand moved down the river, free.

It was the hottest hour of the afternoon. Everything slept: the man buried in the sand, the arbors over the little jetties, the deserted bridges, the houses rising, windows shuttered, above the embankments. The river was low, but the barge, driven by the current, skirted the muddy shoals which rose now and then; otherwise, a light bump on the bottom was enough to send it back into the flow of water, gradually becoming deeper.

One of these bumps made Marcovaldo open his eyes. He saw the sky charged with sunlight, the low summer clouds passing. "How they run," he thought, of the clouds, "and there isn't a breath of wind!" Then he saw some electric wires: they too were running, like the clouds. He looked to one side, as much as he could, with the hundredweight of sand on top of him. The right bank was far away, green, and

it was running; the left was gray, far off, also in flight. He
realized he was in the midst of the river, voyaging. Nobody
answered: he was alone, buried on a sand barge, adrift,
without oars or rudder. He knew he should get up, try to
land, call for help; but at the same time the thought that
sand-packs require absolute immobility held him, made
him feel committed to stay there as long as he could, so as
not to lose precious instants of his cure.

At that moment he saw the bridge; and from the statues
and lamps that adorned the railings, from the breadth of the
arches that touched the sky, he recognized it: he hadn't
realized how far he had come. And as he entered the opaque
region of shade that the arches cast, he remembered the
rapids. About a hundred yards beyond the bridge, the river-
bed made a drop; the barge would drop down the falls and
overturn, and he would be smothered by the sand, the
water, the barge, with no hope of emerging alive. Still, even
at that moment, his greatest concern was the sand cure,
whose beneficent effects would be promptly lost.

He waited for the plunge. And it came: but it was a thud
coming upwards from below. On the brink of the falls, in
that dry season, shoals of mud had collected, some greening
with slender clumps of cane and rushes. The barge ran
aground, on all its flat keel, flinging up the whole load of
sand and the man buried in it. Marcovaldo found himself
hurled into the air as if by a catapult, and at that moment he
saw the river below him. Or rather: he didn't see it at all, he
saw only the teeming crowd of people who filled the river.

On this Saturday afternoon, a great throng of swimmers
crowded that stretch of river, where the shallow water came
only up to the navel; children wallowed in it, whole classes
of them, and fat women, and gentlemen who did the dead-
man's float, and girls in bikinis, and young toughs who
wrestled with each other, and mattresses, balls, life-savers,
inner-tubes, row boats, kayaks, rubber boats, motor boats,
life-saving boats, yawls from yacht clubs, fishermen with
nets, fishermen with rods, old women with parasols, young

ladies in straw hats, and dogs, dogs, dogs, from toy poodles to Saint Bernards: you couldn't see even an inch of the river's surface. And Marcovaldo, as he flew, was uncertain whether he would fall onto a rubber mattress or into the arms of a Junoesque matron, but of one thing he was certain: not even a drop of water would touch him.

AUTUMN

7. *The lunch-box*

The joys of that round and flat vessel, or lunch-box, known as the "pietanziera", consist first of all in its having a screw-on top. The action of unscrewing the cover already makes your mouth water, especially if you don't yet know what is inside, because, for example, it's your wife who prepares the vessel for you every morning. Once the box is uncovered, you see your food packed there: salami and lentils, or hard-boiled eggs and beets, or else polenta and codfish, all neatly arranged within that circumference as the continents and oceans are set on the maps of the globe; and even if the food is scant it gives the effect of being substantial and compact. The cover, once it has been removed, serves as a plate, and so there are two receptacles and you can begin to divide the contents.

Marcovaldo, the handyman, having unscrewed the lid of his box and swiftly inhaled its aroma, grabs the cutlery that he has always carried in his pocket, wrapped in a bundle, ever since he began eating his noon meal from the lunch-box instead of returning home. The fork's first jabs serve to rouse those benumbed victuals a bit, to give the prominence and attraction of a dish just set on the table to those foods that have been cramped inside there for so many hours. Then you begin to see that there isn't much, and you think:

"Best to eat it slowly." But, rapid and ravenous, the first forkfuls have already been raised to the mouth.

The immediate sensation is the sadness of eating cold food, but the joys promptly begin again as you find the flavors of the family board transported to an unusual setting. Marcovaldo has now begun chewing slowly: he is seated on a bench by an avenue, near the place where he works; since his house is far away and to go there at noon costs time and tram tickets, he brings his lunch in the box, bought for the purpose, and he eats in the open air, watching the people go by, and then he refreshes himself at a drinking fountain. If it's autumn and the sun is out, he chooses places where an occasional ray strikes; the shiny red leaves that fall from the trees serve him as napkins; the salami skins go to stray dogs, who are quick to become his friends; and the sparrows collect the bread crumbs, at a moment when no one is going past in the avenue.

As he eats, he thinks: "Why am I so happy to taste the flavor of my wife's cooking here, when at home, among the quarrels and tears, the debts that crop up in every conversation, I can't enjoy it?" And then he thinks: "Now I remember. These are the leftovers from last night's supper." And he is immediately seized again by discontent, perhaps because he has to eat leftovers, cold and a bit soured, perhaps because the aluminum of the lunch-box gives the food a metallic taste, but the notion lodged in his head is: The thought of Domitilla manages to spoil my meals even when I'm far away from her.

At that point, he realizes he has come almost to the end, and again this dish seems to him something very special and rare, and he eats with enthusiasm and devotion the final remains on the bottom of the plate, the ones that taste most of metal. Then, gazing at the empty, greasy receptacle, he is again overcome by sadness.

Then he wraps everything up, puts it in his pocket, and stands; it's still early to go back to work; in the big pocket of his heavy jacket the cutlery drums against the empty lunch-box. Marcovaldo goes to a wine-shop and has them pour him a glass, filled to the brim; or else to a café where he sips a little cup of coffee; then he looks at the pastries in the glass case, the boxes of candies and nougat, persuades himself that he doesn't want any, that he doesn't want anything at all; for a moment he watches the table-football to convince himself that he wants to kill time, not appetite. He goes back into the street. The trams are crowded again; it is almost the hour to return to work, and he heads in that direction.

It so happened that his wife, Domitilla, for personal reasons, bought a great quantity of sausage and turnips. And for three evenings in a row, Marcovaldo found sausage and turnips for supper. Now that sausage must have been made of dog meat; the smell alone was enough to kill your appetite. As for the turnips, this pale and shifty vegetable was the only one Marcovaldo had never been able to bear.

At noon, there they were again: his sausage and turnips, cold and greasy, in the lunch-box. Forgetful as he was, he always unscrewed the lid with curiosity and gluttony, never remembering what he had eaten for supper the previous night; and every day brought the same disappointment. The fourth day, he stuck his fork into it, sniffed once again, rose from the bench, and holding the open lunch-box in his hand, walked absently along the street. The passers-by saw this man carrying a fork in one hand and a plate of sausage in the other, apparently unable to bring himself to raise the first forkful to his mouth.

From a window a voice said: "Hey, mister!"

Marcovaldo raised his eyes. On the mezzanine floor of a grand villa, a boy was standing at a window, his elbows on the sill, where a dish had been set.

"Hey, mister! What are you eating?"

"Sausage and turnips!"

"Lucky you," the boy said.

"Mmm . . ." Marcovaldo replied, vaguely.

"Imagine! I'm supposed to eat fried brains . . ."

Marcovaldo looked at the dish on the sill. There were fried brains, soft and curly as a pile of clouds. His nostrils twitched.

"What? Don't you like brains?" he asked the little boy.

"No. They locked me up in here to punish me, because I wouldn't eat it. But I'll throw it out of the window."

"And you like sausage?"

"Oh, yes, it looks like a snake . . . We never eat it at our house . . ."

"Then you give me your plate and I'll give you mine."

"Hurrah!" The child was overjoyed. He held out to the man his porcelain plate with heavy silver fork, and the man gave him the lunch-box with the tin fork.

And so both fell to eating: the boy at the window-sill and Marcovaldo seated on a bench opposite, both licking their lips and declaring they had never tasted such good food.

But then, behind the boy, a governess appears, with her hands on her hips.

"Well, young man! My goodness! What are you eating?"

"Sausage!" the boy says.

"And who gave it to you?"

"That gentleman there," and he pointed to Marcovaldo, who interrupted his slow and earnest chewing of a morsel of brains.

"Throw it away! The smell! Throw it away!"

"But it's good . . ."

"And your plate? The fork?"

"The gentleman has them . . ." and he pointed again to Marcovaldo, who was holding the fork in the air with a bit of half-eaten brains stuck on it.

The woman began yelling. "Thief! Thief! The silver!"

Marcovaldo stood up, looked for another moment at the half-finished dish of fried brains, went to the window, set plate and fork on the sill, stared at the governess with contempt, and withdrew. He heard the clatter of the lunch-box on the pavement, the boy's crying, the rude slam of the window. He bent to pick up the lunch-box and its cover. They were a bit dented; the cover no longer fit properly. He jammed everything into his pocket and went off to work.

WINTER

8. The forest on the superhighway

Cold has a thousand shapes and a thousand ways of moving in the world: on the sea it gallops like a troop of horses, on the countryside it falls like a swarm of locusts, in the cities like a knife-blade it slashes the streets and penetrates the chinks of unheated houses. In Marcovaldo's house that evening they had burned the last kindling, and the family, all bundled in overcoats, was watching the embers fade in the stove, and the little clouds rise from their own mouths at every breath. They had stopped talking; the little clouds spoke for them: the wife emitted great long ones like sighs, the children puffed them out like assorted soap-bubbles, and Marcovaldo blew them upwards in jerks, like flashes of genius that promptly vanish.

In the end Marcovaldo made up his mind: "I'm going to look for wood. Who knows? I might find some." He stuffed four or five newspapers between his shirt and his jacket as breastplates against gusts of air, he hid a long, snaggle-tooth saw under his overcoat, and thus he went out into the night, followed by the long, hopeful looks of his family. He made a papery rustle at every step; the saw peeped out now and then above his collar.

Looking for wood in the city: easier said than done! Marcovaldo headed at once towards a little patch of public park that stood between two streets. All was deserted.

36

Marcovaldo studied the naked trees, one by one, thinking of his family, waiting for him with their teeth chattering.

Little Michelino, his teeth chattering, was reading a book of fairy-tales, borrowed from the small library at school. The book told of a child, son of a woodsman, who went out with a hatchet to chop wood in the forest. "That's the place to go!" Michelino said. "The forest! There's wood there, all right!" Born and raised in the city, he had never seen a forest, not even at a distance.

Then and there, he worked it out with his brothers: one took a hatchet, one a hook, one a rope; they said good-bye to their Mamma and went out in search of a forest.

They walked around the city, illuminated by street-lamps, and they saw only houses: not a sign of a forest. They encountered an occasional passer-by, but they didn't dare ask him where a forest was. And so they reached the area where the houses of the city ended and the street turned into a highway.

At the sides of the highway, the children saw the forest: a thick growth of strange trees blocked the view of the plain. Their trunks were very very slender, erect or slanting; and their crowns were flat and outspread, revealing the strangest shapes and the strangest colors when a passing car illuminated them with its headlights. Boughs in the form of a toothpaste tube, a face, cheese, hand, razor, bottle, cow, tire, all dotted with a foliage of letters of the alphabet.

"Hurrah!" Michelino said. "This is the forest!"

And, spellbound, the brothers watched the moon rise among those strange shadows: "How beautiful it is . . ."

Michelino immediately reminded them of their purpose in coming there: wood. So they chopped down a little tree in the form of a yellow primrose blossom, cut it into bits, and took it home.

Marcovaldo came home with his scant armful of damp branches, and found the stove burning.

"Where did you find it?" he cried, pointing to what

remained of a billboard, which, being of plywood, had burned very quickly.

"In the forest!" the children said.

"What forest?"

"The one by the highway. It's full of wood!"

Since it was so simple, and there was need of more wood, he thought he might as well follow the children's example, and Marcovaldo again went out with his saw. He went to the highway.

Officer Astolfo, of the highway police, was a bit short-sighted, and on night duty, racing on his motorcycle, he should have worn eyeglasses; but he didn't say so, for fear it would block his advancement.

That evening, there was a report that on the super-highway a bunch of kids was knocking down billboards. Officer Astolfo set out to inspect.

On either side of the road, the forest of strange figures, admonishing and gesticulating, accompanied Astolfo, who peered at them one by one, widening his near-sighted eyes. There, in the beam of his motorcycle's headlight, he caught a little urchin who had climbed up on a billboard. Astolfo put on the brakes. "Hey, what are you doing there? Jump down this minute!" The kid didn't move and stuck out its tongue. Astolfo approached and saw it was an ad for processed cheese, with a big child licking his lips. "Yes, of course," Astolfo said, and zoomed off.

A little later, in the shadow of a huge billboard, he illuminated a sad, frightened face. "Don't make a move! Don't try running away!" But nobody ran away. It was a suffering human face painted in the midst of a foot covered with corns: an ad for a corn-remover. "Oh, sorry," Astolfo said, and dashed away.

The billboard for a headache tablet was a gigantic head of a man, his hands over his eyes, in pain. Astolfo sped past, and the headlight illuminated Marcovaldo, who had scrambled to the top with his saw, trying to cut off a slice. Dazzled by the light, Marcovaldo huddled down and remained motionless, clinging to an ear of the big head, where the saw had already reached the middle of the brow.

Astolfo examined it carefully and said: "Oh, yes. Stappa tablets! Very effective ad! Smart idea! That little man up there with the saw represents the migraine that is cutting the head in two. I got it right away!" And he went off, content.

All was silence and cold. Marcovaldo heaved a sigh of relief, settled on his uncomfortable perch, and resumed work. The muffled scrape of the saw against the wood spread through the moonlit sky.

SPRING

9. The good air

"These children," the Public Health doctor said, "need to breathe some good air, at a certain altitude; they should run through meadows . . ."

He was between the beds of the half-basement where the family lived, and was pressing his stethoscope against little Teresa's back, between her shoulder-blades, frail as the wings of a tiny featherless bird. The beds were two, and the four children, all ill, peeked out at the head and foot of each bed, with flushed cheeks and glistening eyes.

"On meadows like the flower-bed in the square?" Michelino asked.

"The altitude of a skyscraper?" asked Filippetto.

"Air that's good to eat?" asked Pietruccio.

Marcovaldo, tall and skinny, and his wife, Domitilla, short and squat, were leaning on one elbow on either side of a rickety chest of drawers. Without moving the elbow, each raised the other arm and then dropped it, grumbling together: "Where are we supposed to find those things, six mouths to feed, loaded with debts? How are we supposed to manage?"

"The most beautiful place we can send them," Marcovaldo declared, "is into the streets."

"We'll find good air," Domitilla concluded, "when we're evicted and have to sleep under the stars."

One Saturday afternoon, as soon as they were well again, Marcovaldo took the children and led them off on a walk in the hills. The part of the city where they lived is the farthest from the hills. To reach the slopes they made a long journey on a crowded tram and the children saw only the legs of passengers around them. Little by little the tram emptied; at the windows, finally freed, an avenue appeared, climbing up. And so they reached the end of the line and set forth.

It was early spring; the trees were just budding in a tepid sun. The children looked around, slightly disoriented. Marcovaldo led them up a little path of steps, rising among the green.

"Why is there a stairway without a house over it?" Michelino asked.

"It's not a house stairway; it's like a street."

"A street . . . And how can the cars manage the steps?"

Around them there were garden walls, with trees inside.

"Walls without a roof . . . Did they bomb them?"

"They're gardens . . . like courtyards . . ." the father explained. "The house is farther back, beyond those trees."

Michelino shook his head, unconvinced. "But courtyards are inside houses, not outside."

Teresina asked: "Do the trees live in these houses?"

As they climbed up, it seemed to Marcovaldo that he was gradually shedding the moldy smell of the warehouse in which he shifted packages for eight hours a day and the damp stains on the walls of his house and the dust that settled, gilded, in the cone of light from the little window, and the fits of coughing in the darkness. His children now seemed to him less sallow and frail, already somehow part of that light and that green.

"You like it here, don't you?"

"Yes."

"Why?"

"There aren't any police. You can pull up the flowers, throw stones."

"What about breathing? Are you breathing?"

"No."

"The air's good here."

They chewed it. "What are you talking about? It doesn't have any taste at all."

They climbed almost to the top of the hill. At one turn, the city appeared, way down below, spread flat on the gray cobweb of the streets. The children rolled around on a meadow as if they had never done anything else in their life. A little breeze sprang up; it was already evening. In the city a few lights came on, in a confused sparkle. Marcovaldo felt again a rush of the feeling he had had as a young man, arriving in the city, when those streets, those lights attracted him as if he expected something unknown from them. The swallows plunged headlong through the air onto the city.

Then he was seized by the sadness of having to go back down there, and in the clotted landscape he figured out the shadow of his neighborhood: it seemed to him a leaden wasteland, stagnant, covered by the thick scales of the roofs and the shreds of smoke flapping on the stick-like chimney-pots.

It had turned cool: perhaps he should call the children. But seeing them swinging peacefully on the lower limbs of a tree, he dismissed that thought. Michelino came over to him and asked: "Papà, why don't we come and live here?"

"Stupid, there aren't any houses; nobody lives up here!" Marcovaldo said, with irritation, because he had actually been daydreaming of being able to live up there.

And Michelino said: "Nobody? What about those gentlemen? Look!"

The air was turning gray and down from the meadows came a troop of men, of various ages, all dressed in heavy gray suits, buttoned up like pyjamas, all with cap and cane. They came in bunches, some talking in loud voices or laughing, sticking those canes into the grass or carrying them, hung by the curved handle, over their arm.

"Who are they? Where are they going?" Michelino asked his father, but Marcovaldo was looking at them, silent.

One passed nearby; he was a heavy man of about forty. "Good evening!" he said. "Well, what news do you bring us, from down in the city?"

"Good evening," Marcovaldo said. "What do you mean by news?"

"Nothing. I was just talking," the man said, and stopped; he had a broad, white face, with only a splotch of pink, or red, like a shadow, over his cheekbones. "I always say that, to anybody from the city. I've been up here for three months, you understand."

"And you never go down?"

"Hmph, when the doctors decide to let me!" And he laughed briefly. "And this!" And he tapped his fingers on his chest, with some more brief laughter, a bit breathless. "They've already discharged me twice, as cured, but as soon as I went back to the factory, wham, all over again. And they ship me back up here. Some fun!"

"Them too?" Marcovaldo asked, nodding at the other men, who had scattered over the grass; and at the same time, his eyes sought Filippetto and Teresa and Pietruccio, whom he had lost sight of.

"All comrades on the same holiday," the man said, and winked. "We're let out on a pass, before taps . . . We go to bed early . . . Obviously, we can't go beyond the grounds . . ."

"What grounds?"

"This is part of the sanatorium. Didn't you know?"

Marcovaldo took the hand of Michelino, who had stood there listening, a bit scared. Evening was climbing up the slopes; there below, their neighborhood was no longer discernible, and it seemed not so much to have been swallowed by the shadows, but to have spread its own shadow everywhere. It was time to go back. "Teresa! Filippetto!" Marcovaldo called and started to look for them. "Sorry," he said to the man, "I don't see the other children anywhere."

The man stepped to a parapet. "They're down there," he said, "they're picking cherries."

In a ditch, Marcovaldo saw a cherry tree and around it were the men dressed in gray, pulling down the branches with their curved sticks, and picking the fruit. And Teresa and the two boys, all delighted, were also picking cherries and taking them from the men's hands and laughing with them.

"It's late," Marcovaldo said. "It's cold. Let's go home . . ."

The heavy man pointed the tip of his cane towards the rows of lights that were coming on, down below.

"In the evening," he said, "with this stick I take my walk in the city. I choose a street, a row of lamps, and I follow it, like this . . . I stop at the windows, I meet people, I say hello to them . . . When you walk in the city, think of it sometimes: my cane is following you . . ."

The children came back crowned with leaves, made by the inmates.

"This is a wonderful place, Papà!" Teresa said. "We'll come and play here again, won't we?"

"Papà!" Michelino blurted. "Why don't we come and live here, too, with these gentlemen?"

"It's late. Say good-bye to the gentlemen! Say thanks for the cherries. Come on! We're going!"

They headed home. They were tired. Marcovaldo didn't answer any questions. Filippetto wanted to be carried, Pietruccio wanted to ride piggy-back, Teresa made him drag her by the hand, and Michelino, the oldest, went ahead by himself, kicking stones.

SUMMER

10. A journey with the cows

The city noises that on summer nights come through the open windows into the rooms of those who are made sleepless by the heat, the true noises of the night-time city, are audible at a certain hour, when the anonymous din of motors dies away and is silent, and from the silence, discreet, distinct, graduated according to the distance, emerge the step of a noctambulant, the rustle of a night watchman's bike, a remote muddled brawl, and a snoring from the upper floors, the groan of a sick man, the continued striking of an old clock every hour. Until, at dawn, the orchestra of alarm clocks in the working-class houses tunes up, and a tram goes by on its tracks.

And so, one night, between his wife and the children all sweating in their sleep, Marcovaldo lay with his eyes closed, to listen to as much of this powdering of frail sounds as filtered from the pavement down through the low windows into his half-basement. He heard the swift, cheerful heel of a woman who was late, the patched sole of the man who stopped irregularly to collect cigarette butts, the whistle of someone who felt alone, and every now and then a broken clash of words in a dialogue between friends, enough to suggest they were talking about sports or money. But in the hot night those sounds lost all relief, they dissolved as if dampened by the sultry heat that crammed

45

the void of the streets, and yet they seemed to want to impose themselves, to assert their dominion over that uninhabited realm. In every human presence Marcovaldo recognized sadly a brother, stuck like him, even in vacation time, to that oven of cooked and dusty cement, by debts, by the burden of the family, by the meagerness of his wages.

And as if the impossible thought of vacation had suddenly opened the gates of a dream to him, he seemed to hear a distant clank of bells, and a dog's bark, and also a brief lowing. But his eyes were open, he wasn't dreaming: and, pricking up his ears, he sought to regain a grip on those vague impressions, or a denial of them; and he actually did hear a sound as of hundreds and hundreds of steps, slow, scattered, hollow, which came closer and drowned out all other sounds, except, indeed, that rusty clanking.

Marcovaldo got up, slipped on his shirt and trousers. "Where are you going?" asked his wife, who slept with one eye open.

"There's a herd of cattle passing in the street. I'm going to see it."

"Me, too! Me, too!" cried the children, who knew how to wake up at the right moment.

It was the sort of herd that used to cross the city at night, in early summer, going towards the mountains for the alpine pasture. Climbing into the street with their eyes still half-closed in sleep, the children saw the stream of dun or piebald withers which invaded the sidewalk, brushed against the walls covered with bills, the lowered shutters, the stakes of no-parking signs, the gasoline pumps. Cautiously extending their hoofs from the step at the intersections, their muzzles never betraying a jolt of curiosity, pressed against the loins of those ahead of them, the cows brought with them the odor of dung, wild flowers, milk and the languid sound of their bells, and the city seemed not to touch them, already absorbed as they were into their world of damp meadows, mountain mists and the fords of streams.

Impatient, on the contrary, as if made nervous by the looming city, the cowherds wore themselves out in brief, futile dashes along the side of the line, raising their sticks and bursting out in broken, guttural cries. The dogs, to whom nothing human is alien, made a display of nonchalance, proceeding with noses erect, little bells tinkling, intent on their job; but clearly they too were uneasy and restless, otherwise they would have allowed themselves to be distracted and would have begun sniffing corners, lampposts, stains on the pavement, as is every city dog's first thought.

"Papà," the children said. "Are cows like trams? Do they have stops? Where's the beginning of the cows' line?"

"There's no connection between them and trams," Marcovaldo explained. "They're going to the mountains."

"Can they wear skis?" Pietruccio asked.

"They're going to pasture, to eat grass."

"Don't they get fined if they trample the lawns?"

The only one not asking questions was Michelino, who, older than the others, already had his own ideas about cows, and was now intent simply on checking them, observing the mild horns, the withers, and variegated coats. And so he followed the herd, trotting along at its side like the sheep dogs.

When the last group had passed, Marcovaldo took the children's hands to go back to sleep, but he couldn't see Michelino. He went down into the room and asked his wife: "Has Michelino already come home?"

"Michelino? Wasn't he with you?"

"He started following the herd, and God only knows where he's got to," Marcovaldo thought, and ran back to the street. The herd had already crossed the square, and Marcovaldo had to look for the street it had turned into. But that night, it seemed, various herds were crossing the city, each along

a different street, each heading for its own valley.
Marcovaldo tracked down and overtook one herd, then
realized it wasn't his; at an intersection he saw, four streets
farther on, another herd proceeding along a parallel, and he
ran that way; there, the cowherds told him they had met
another heading in the opposite direction. And so, until the
last sound of a cow-bell had died away in the dawn light,
Marcovaldo went on combing the city in vain.

The captain to whom he went to report his son's dis-
appearance said: "Followed a herd of cows? He's prob-
ably gone off to the mountains, for a summer holiday,
lucky kid. Don't worry: he'll come back all tanned and
fattened up."

The captain's opinion was confirmed a few days later by
a clerk in the place where Marcovaldo worked who had
returned from his first-shift holiday. At a mountain pass he
had encountered the boy: he was with the herd, he sent
greetings to his father, and he was fine.

In the dusty city heat Marcovaldo kept thinking of his
lucky son, who now was surely spending his hours in a fir
tree's shade, whistling with a wisp of grass in his mouth,
looking down at the cows moving slowly over the meadow,
and listening to a murmur of waters in the shadows of the
valley.

His Mamma, on the contrary, couldn't wait for him
to return: "Will he come back by train? By bus? It's been
a week . . . It's been a month . . . The weather must be
bad . . ." And she could find no peace, even though having
one fewer at table every day was in itself a relief.

"Lucky kid, up in the cool, stuffing himself with butter
and cheese," Marcovaldo said, and every time, at the end of
the street, there appeared, in a light haze, the jagged white
and gray of the mountains, he felt as if he had sunk into a
well, in whose light, up at the top, he seemed to see maple
and chestnut fronds glinting, and to hear wild bees buzzing,
and Michelino up there, lazy and happy, amid milk and
honey and blackberry thickets.

But he too was expecting his son's return evening after evening, though, unlike the boy's mother, he wasn't thinking of the schedules of trains and buses: he was listening at night to the footsteps on the street as if the little window of the room were the mouth of a seashell, re-echoing, when you put your ear to it, the sounds of the mountain.

One night he sat abruptly up in bed: it wasn't an illusion; he heard approaching on the cobbles that unmistakable trample of cloven hoofs, mixed with the tinkling of bells.

They ran to the street, he and the whole family. The herd was returning, slow and grave. And in the midst of the herd, astride a cow's back, his hands clutching its collar, his head bobbing at every step, was Michelino, half asleep.

They lifted him down, a dead weight; they hugged and kissed him. He was dazed.

"How are you? Was it beautiful?"

"Oh . . . yes . . ."

"Were you homesick?"

"Yes . . ."

"Is it beautiful in the mountains?"

He was standing, facing them, his brows knit, his gaze hard.

"I worked like a mule," he said, and spat on the ground. He now had a man's face. "Carrying the buckets to the milkers every evening, from one cow to the next, and then emptying them into the cans, in a hurry, always in a worse hurry, until late. And then early in the morning, rolling the cans down to the trucks that take them to the city. And counting . . . always counting: the cows, the cans, and if you made a mistake there was trouble . . ."

"But weren't you in the meadows? When the cows were grazing?"

"There was never enough time. Always something to be done. The milk, the bedding, the dung. And all for what? With the excuse that I didn't have a work-contract, what did they pay me? Practically nothing. But if you think I'm going to hand it over to you now, you're wrong. Come on, let's go to sleep; I'm dead tired."

He shrugged, blew his nose, and went into the house.

The herd was still moving away along the street, carrying with it the lying, languid odor of hay and the sound of bells.

AUTUMN

11. The poisonous rabbit

When the day comes to leave the hospital, you already know it in the morning and if you're in good shape you move around the wards, practising the way you're going to walk when you're outside; you whistle, act like a well man with those still sick, not to arouse envy but for the pleasure of adopting a tone of encouragement. You see the sun beyond the big panes, or the fog if there's fog; you hear the sounds of the city; and everything is different from before, when every morning you felt them enter – the light and sound of an unattainable world – as you woke behind the bars of that bed. Now, outside, there is your world again. The healed man recognizes it as natural and usual; and suddenly he notices once more the smell of the hospital.

Marcovaldo, one morning, was sniffing around like that, cured, waiting for them to write certain things in his health insurance book so that he could leave. The doctor took his papers, said to him, "Wait here", and left him alone in the office. Marcovaldo looked at the white-enameled furniture he had so hated, the test-tubes full of grim substances, and tried to cheer himself with the thought that he was about to leave it all. But he couldn't manage to feel the joy he would have expected. Perhaps it was the idea of going back to the warehouse to shift packing cases, or of the mischief his children had surely been up to in his absence, and especially

51

of the fog outside that made him think of having to step out into the void, to dissolve in a damp nothingness. And so he looked around, with a vague need to feel affection towards something in here; but everything he saw reminded him of torture or discomfort.

Then he saw a rabbit in a cage. It was a white rabbit, with a long, fluffy coat, a pink triangle of a nose, amazed red eyes, ears almost furless flattened against its back. It wasn't all that big, but in the narrow cage its crouching oval body made the wire screen bulge and clumps of fur stuck out, ruffled by a slight trembling. Outside the cage, on the table, there was some grass and the remains of a carrot. Marcovaldo thought of how unhappy the animal must be, shut up in there, seeing that carrot but not being able to eat it. And he opened the door of the cage. The rabbit didn't come out: it stayed there, still, with only a slight twitch of its face, as if it were pretending to chew in order to seem nonchalant. Marcovaldo took the carrot and held it closer, then slowly drew it back, to urge the rabbit to come out. The rabbit followed him, cautiously bit the carrot and began gnawing it diligently, in Marcovaldo's hand. The man stroked it on the back and, meanwhile, squeezed it, to see if it was fat. He felt it was somewhat bony, under its coat. From this fact, and from the way it pulled on the carrot, it was obvious that they kept it on short rations. If it belonged to me, Marcovaldo thought, I would stuff it until it became a ball. And he looked at it with the loving eye of the breeder who manages to allow kindness towards the animal to coexist with anticipation of the roast, all in one emotion. There, after days and days of sordid stay in the hospital, at the moment of leaving, he discovered a friendly presence, which would have sufficed to fill his hours and his thoughts. And he had to leave it, go back into the foggy city, where you don't encounter rabbits.

The carrot was almost finished. Marcovaldo took the animal into his arms while he looked around for something else to feed him. He held its nose to a potted geranium on the doctor's desk, but the animal indicated it didn't like the plant. At that same moment Marcovaldo heard the doctor's step, coming back: how could he explain why he was holding the rabbit in his arms? He was wearing his heavy work coat, tight at the waist. In a hurry, he stuck the rabbit inside, buttoned his coat all the way up, and to keep the doctor from seeing that wriggling bulge at his stomach, he shifted it around to his back. The rabbit, frightened, behaved itself. Marcovaldo collected his papers and moved the rabbit to his chest, because he had to turn and leave. And so, with the rabbit hidden under his coat, he left the hospital and went to work.

"Ah, you're cured at last?" the foreman, Signor Viligelmo, said, seeing him arrive. "And what's that growth there?" and he pointed to the bulging chest.

"I'm wearing a hot poultice to prevent cramps," Marcovaldo said.

At that, the rabbit twitched, and Marcovaldo jumped up like an epileptic.

"Now what's come over you?" Viligelmo said.

"Nothing. Hiccups," he answered, and with one hand he shoved the rabbit behind his back.

"You're still a bit seedy, I notice," the boss said.

The rabbit was trying to crawl up his back, and Marcovaldo shrugged hard to send it down again.

"You're shivering. Go home for another day. And make sure you're well tomorrow."

Marcovaldo came home, carrying the rabbit by its ears, like a lucky hunter.

"Papà! Papà!" the children hailed him, running to meet him. "Where did you catch it? Can we have it? Is it a present for us?" And they tried to grab it at once.

"You're back?" his wife said, and from the look she gave him, Marcovaldo realized that his period of hospitalization had served only to enable her to accumulate new grievances against him. "A live animal? What are you going to do with it? It'll make messes all over the place."

Marcovaldo cleared the table and set the rabbit down in the middle, where it huddled flat, as if trying to vanish. "Don't anybody dare touch it!" he said. "This is our rabbit, and it's going to fatten up peacefully till Christmas."

"Is it a male or a female?" Michelino asked.

Marcovaldo had given no thought to the possibility of its being a female. A new plan immediately occurred to him: if it was a female, he could mate her and start raising rabbits. And already in his imagination the damp walls disappeared and the room was a green farm among the fields.

But it was a male, all right. Still Marcovaldo had now got this idea of raising rabbits into his head. It was a male, but a very handsome male, for whom a bride should be found and the means to raise a family.

"What are we going to feed it, when we don't have enough for ourselves?" his wife asked, sharply.

"Let me give it some thought," Marcovaldo said.

The next day, at work, from some green potted plants in the Management Office, which he was supposed to take out every morning, water, then put back, he removed one leaf each—broad leaves, shiny on one side and opaque on the other—and stuck them into his overalls. Then, when one of the girls came in with a bunch of flowers, he asked her, "Did your boy-friend give them to you? Aren't you going to give me one?" and he pocketed that, too. To a boy peeling a pear, he said, "Leave me the peel." And so, a leaf here, a peeling there, a petal somewhere else, he hoped to feed the animal.

At a certain point, Signor Viligelmo sent for him. Can they have noticed the plants are missing leaves? Marcovaldo wondered, accustomed always to feeling guilty.

In the foreman's office there was the doctor from the hospital, two Red Cross men, and a city policeman. "Listen," the doctor said, "a rabbit has disappeared from my laboratory. If you know anything about it, you'd better not try to act smart. Because we've injected it with the germs of a terrible disease and it can spread it through the whole city. I needn't ask if you've eaten it; if you had, you'd be dead and gone by now."

An ambulance was waiting outside; they rushed and got in it, and with the siren screaming constantly, they went through streets and avenues to Marcovaldo's house, and along the way there remained a wake of leaves and peelings and flowers that Marcovaldo sadly threw out of the window.

Marcovaldo's wife that morning simply didn't know what to put in the pot. She looked at the rabbit her husband had brought home the day before, now in a makeshift cage, filled with shavings. "It arrived just at the right moment," she said to herself. "There's no money; his wages have already gone for the extra medicines the Public Health doesn't cover; the shops won't give us any more credit. Raise rabbits, indeed! Or wait till Christmas to roast it! We're skipping meals, and we're supposed to fatten a rabbit!"

"Isolina," she said to her daughter, "you're a big girl now, you have to learn how to cook a rabbit. You begin by killing it and skinning it, and then I'll tell you what to do next."

Isolina was reading a magazine of sentimental romances. "No," she whined, "*you* begin by killing it and skinning it, and then I'll watch how you cook it."

"What a help!" her mother said. "I don't have the heart to kill it. But I know it's a very easy matter; you just have to hold it by the ears and hit it hard on the back of the head. As for skinning, we'll see."

"We won't see anything," the daughter said, without raising her nose from the magazine. "I'm not hitting a live rabbit on the head. And I haven't the slightest notion of skinning it, either."

The three little ones had listened to this dialogue with wide eyes.

Their mother pondered for a moment, looked at them, then said, "Children . . ."

The children, as if by agreement, turned their backs on their mother and left the room.

"Wait, children!" their mother said. "I wanted to ask you if you'd like to take the rabbit outside. We'll tie a pretty ribbon around his neck and you can go for a walk with him."

The children stopped and exchanged looks. "A walk where?" Michelino asked.

"Oh, a little stroll. Then go call on Signora Diomira, show her the rabbit, and ask her if she'll please kill it and skin it for us. She's so good at that."

The mother had found the right method: children, as everyone knows, are caught up by the thing they like most, and they prefer not to think of the rest. And so they found a long, lilac-colored ribbon, tied it around the animal's neck, and used it as a leash, fighting over it, and pulling after them the reluctant, half-strangled rabbit.

"Tell Signora Diomira," the mother insisted, "that she can keep a leg for herself! No, better the head. Oh, she can take her pick."

The children had barely gone out when Marcovaldo's room was surrounded and invaded by orderlies, doctors, guards, and policemen. Marcovaldo was in their midst, more dead than alive. "Where is the rabbit that was taken from the hospital? Hurry: show us where it is, but don't touch it; it's infected with the germs of a terrible disease!" Marcovaldo led them to the cage, but it was empty. "Already eaten?" "No, no!" "Where is it then?" "At Signora Diomira's!" And the pursuers resumed their hunt.

They knocked at Signora Diomira's door. "Rabbit? What rabbit? Are you crazy?" Seeing her house invaded by strangers, in white jackets or uniforms, looking for a rabbit, the old woman nearly had a stroke. She knew nothing about Marcovaldo's rabbit.

In fact, the three children, trying to save the rabbit from death, had decided to take it to a safe place, play with it for a while, and then let it go; and instead of stopping at Signora

Diomira's landing, they decided to climb up to a terrace over the rooftops. They would tell their mother it had broken the leash and had run off. But no animal seemed so ill-suited to an escape as that rabbit. Making it climb all those steps was a problem: it huddled, frightened, on each step. In the end they picked it up and carried it.

On the terrace they wanted to make it run: it wouldn't run. They tried setting it on the edge of the roof, to see if it would walk the way cats do; but it seemed to suffer vertigo. They tried hoisting it onto a TV antenna, to see if it could keep its balance: no, it fell down. Bored, the children ripped away the leash, turned the animal loose at a place where all the paths of the roofs opened out, an oblique and angular sea, and they left.

When it was alone, the rabbit began moving. It ventured a few steps, looked around, changed direction, turned, then, in little hops and skips, it started over the roofs. It was an animal born prisoner: its yearning for liberty did not have broad horizons. The greatest gift it had known in life was the ability to have a few moments free of fear. Now, now it could move, with nothing around to frighten it, perhaps for the first time in its life. The place was unfamiliar, but a clear concept of familiar and unfamiliar was something it had never been able to formulate. And ever since it had begun to feel an undefined, mysterious ailment gnawing inside itself, the whole world was of less and less interest to it. And so it went onto the roofs; and the cats that saw it hopping didn't understand what it was and they drew back, in awe.

Meanwhile, from skylights, from dormer windows, from flat decks, the rabbit's itinerary had not gone unremarked. Some people began to display basins of salad on their sills, peeking then from behind the curtains, others threw a pear core on the roof-tiles and spread a string lasso around it, someone else arranged a row of bits of carrot along the parapet, leading to his own window. And a rallying-cry ran through all the families living in the garrets: "Stewed rabbit today" – or "fricasseed rabbit" – or "roast rabbit".

The animal had noticed these lures, these silent offers of food. And though it was hungry, it didn't trust them. It knew that every time humans tried to attract it with offers of food, something obscure and painful happened: either they stuck a syringe into its flesh, or a scalpel, or they forced it into a buttoned-up jacket, or they dragged it along with a ribbon around its neck . . . And the memory of these misfortunes merged with the pain it felt inside, with the slow change of organs that it sensed, with the prescience of death. And hunger. But as if it knew that, of all these discomforts, only hunger could be allayed, and recognized that these treacherous human beings could provide, in addition to cruel sufferings, a sense – which it also needed – of protection, of domestic warmth, it decided to surrender to play the humans' game: then whatever had to happen, would happen. So, it began to eat the bits of carrot, following the trail that, as the rabbit well knew, would make it prisoner and martyr again, but savoring once more, and perhaps for the last time, the good earthy flavor of vegetables. Now it was approaching the garret window, now a hand would stretch out to catch it: instead, all of a sudden, the window slammed and closed it out. This was an event alien to its experience: a trap that refused to snap shut. The rabbit turned, looked for other signs of treachery around, to choose the best one to give in to. But meanwhile the leaves of salad had been drawn indoors, the lassos thrown away, the lurking people had vanished, windows and skylights were now barred, terraces were deserted.

It so happened that a police truck had passed through the city, with a loudspeaker shouting: "Attention, attention! A long-haired white rabbit has been lost; it is affected by a serious, contagious disease! Anyone finding it should be informed that it is poisonous to eat; even its touch can transmit harmful germs! Anyone seeing it should alert the nearest police station, hospital, or fire house!"

Terror spread over the rooftops. Everyone was on guard, and the moment they sighted the rabbit, which, with a limp flop, moved from one roof to the next, they gave the alarm, and all disappeared as if at the approach of a swarm of locusts. The rabbit proceeded, teetering on the cornices; this sense of solitude, just at the moment when it had discovered the necessity of human nearness, seemed even more menacing to it, unbearable.

Meanwhile Cavalier Ulrico, an old hunter, had loaded his rifle with cartridges for hare, and had gone to take his stand on a terrace, hiding behind a chimney. When he saw the white shadow of the rabbit emerge from the fog, he fired; but his emotion at the thought of the animal's evil bane was so great that the spatter of shot fell a bit off the mark onto the tiles, like hail. The rabbit heard the shot rattle all around, and one pellet pierced its ear. It understood: this was a declaration of war; at this point all relations with mankind were broken off. And in its contempt of humans, at what seemed, to the rabbit, somehow a base ingratitude, it decided to end it all.

A roof covered with corrugated iron sloped down, oblique, and ended at the void, in the opaque nothingness of the fog. The rabbit planted itself there on all four paws, first cautiously, then letting itself go. And so, slipping, surrounded and consumed by its pain, it went towards death. At the edge, the drainpipe delayed it for a second, then it tumbled down . . .

And it landed in the gloved hands of a fireman, perched at the top of a portable ladder. Foiled even in that extreme act of animal dignity, the rabbit was bundled into the ambulance, which set off full-tilt towards the hospital. Also aboard were Marcovaldo, his wife, and his children, to be interned for observation and for a series of vaccine tests.

WINTER

12. The wrong stop

For anyone who dislikes his home and finds it inhospitable, the favorite refuge on cold evenings is the movies. Marcovaldo had a passion for Technicolor films on the wide screen, which can embrace the most vast horizons: prairies, rocky mountains, equatorial forests, islands where you live with a garland around your head. He would see the picture twice, and he never came out until they were closing the theater; and in his thoughts he continued living in those landscapes and breathing those colors. But the return home in the drizzling night, the wait at the stop for tram number 30, the realization that his life would know no other setting beyond trams, traffic-lights, rooms in the half-basement, gas stoves, drying laundry, warehouses and shipping rooms, made the film's splendor fade for him to a worn and gray sadness.

That evening, the film he had seen took place in the forests of India: steam rose in clouds from the swampy undergrowth, and serpents slithered along the lianas and climbed up the statues of ancient temples swallowed up by the jungle.

Coming out of the theater, he opened his eyes at the street, closed them again, reopened them: he saw nothing. Absolutely nothing. Not even in front of his nose. In the hours he had spent inside, fog had invaded the city, a thick, opaque fog, which engulfed things and sounds, flattened distances into a space without dimensions, mixed lights into the darkness and transformed them into glows without shape or place.

Marcovaldo headed mechanically for the stop of the 30 tram and banged his nose against the signpost. At that moment he realized he was happy: the fog, erasing the world around him, allowed him to hold in his eyes the visions of the wide screen. Even the cold was muffled, as if the city had pulled a cloud over it, like a blanket. Bundled up in his overcoat, Marcovaldo felt protected from every external sensation, suspended in the void; and he could color this void with the images of India, the Ganges, the jungle, Calcutta.

The tram arrived, evanescent as a phantom, slowly jangling; things existed just to the slight extent that sufficed; for Marcovaldo staying at the rear of the tram that evening, his back to the other passengers, as he stared beyond the panes at the empty night traversed only by undefined luminous presences and by an occasional shadow blacker than the darkness, offered the perfect situation for day-dreaming, for projecting in front of himself, wherever he went, a never-ending film on a boundless screen.

With these fantasies he lost count of the stops; all at once he asked himself where he was; he saw the tram was now almost empty; he peered out of the windows, interpreted the glimmers that surfaced, decided his stop was the next, ran to the door just in time, and got out. He looked around, seeking some reference-point. But the few shadows and lights his eyes could discern refused to form any known image. He had got off at the wrong stop and didn't know where he was.

If he met a passer-by it would be easy to ask him the way; but whether because of the loneliness of this place or because of the hour or the bad weather, there wasn't a shadow of a human being to be seen. Finally he saw one, a shadow, and waited for it to come closer. No, it was moving away; perhaps it was crossing the street, or walking down the middle of it; it might not be a pedestrian, but a cyclist, on a bicycle without a headlight.

Marcovaldo cried out: "Hey! Hey, mister! Please, can you tell me where Via Pancrazio Pancrazietti is?"

The shape moved farther away, was now almost invisible. "That way . . ." But there was no telling which way he had pointed.

"Right or left?" shouted Marcovaldo, but he could have been addressing the void.

An answer came, the wake of an answer: ". . . eft!" but it could also have been ". . . ight!" In any case, since there was no seeing which way the other man faced, right and left meant nothing.

Now Marcovaldo was walking towards a glow that seemed to come from the opposite sidewalk, a bit farther on. But the distance proved to be much greater: he had to cross a kind of square, with a little island of grass in the middle, and arrows (the only intelligible sign) indicating that traffic had to keep right. It was late, but surely some café was still open, some tavern; the sign he was just beginning to decipher said: Bar . . . Then it went out; on what must have been an illuminated window a shaft of darkness fell, like a blind. The bar was closing, and it was still—he seemed to understand at that moment—very far away.

So he might as well head for another light. As he walked, Marcovaldo didn't know if he was following a straight line, if the luminous dot he was now heading for was always the same or had doubled or trebled or changed position. The soot, a somewhat milky black, within which he moved was so fine that already he felt it infiltrating his overcoat, as if through a sieve, between the threads of the cloth, which soaked it up like a sponge.

The light he reached was the smoky entrance to a tavern. Inside, there were people seated or standing at the counter, but, because of the poor illumination or because the fog had penetrated everywhere, even here forms seemed blurred, like certain taverns you see in the movies, situated in ancient times or in distant lands.

"I was looking . . . maybe you gentlemen know where it is . . . for Via Pancrazietti . . ." he began saying, but there was noise in the tavern, drunks who laughed, believing him drunk, and the questions he managed to ask, the explanations he managed to obtain, were also foggy and blurred. Especially since, to warm himself, he ordered—or rather, he allowed the men standing at the counter to force on him – a quarter-liter of wine, at first, and then another half-liter, plus a few glasses which, with great slaps on the back, were offered him by the others. In short, when he came out of the tavern, his notions of the way home were no clearer than before, though, in compensation, the fog was more than ever capable of containing all continents and colors.

With the warmth of the wine inside him, Marcovaldo walked for a good quarter of an hour, with steps that constantly felt the need of stretching to the left and to the right, to gauge the width of the sidewalk (if he was still following a sidewalk), and hands that felt the need to touch continuously the walls (if he was still following a wall). The fog in his thoughts, as he walked, was gradually dispelled; but the fog outside remained dense. He remembered that at the tavern they had told him to take a certain avenue, follow it for a hundred yards, then ask again. But now he didn't know how far he had come from the tavern, or if he had only walked around the block.

The spaces seemed uninhabited, within brick walls like the confines of factories. At one corner there was surely the marble plaque with the name of the street, but the light of the lamp-post, suspended between the two lanes, didn't reach that far. To approach the words, Marcovaldo climbed up a no-parking sign. He climbed until he could put his nose on the plaque, but the letters had faded and he had no matches to illuminate them better. Above the plaque, the wall ended in a flat, broad top, and leaning out from the no-parking sign, Marcovaldo managed to hoist himself up there. He had glimpsed, set above the top of the wall, a big whitish sign. He took a few steps along the top of the wall, reaching the sign; here the street-light illuminated the black letters on the white ground, but the words: "Access to unauthorized persons strictly prohibited" gave him no enlightenment.

The top of the wall was so wide that he could balance himself on it and walk; indeed, when he thought about it, it was better than the sidewalk, because the street-lights were high enough to illuminate his steps, making a bright stripe in the midst of the darkness. At a certain point the wall ended and Marcovaldo found himself against the capital of a gate-post. No: the wall made a right angle and went on . . .

And so, what with angles, niches, junctures, posts, Marcovaldo's route followed an irregular pattern; several times he thought the wall was ending, then discovered it continued in another direction; after so many turns he no longer knew what direction he was headed in, or rather, on which side he should jump, if he wanted to move down to the street. Jump . . . And what if the height had increased? He crouched on the top of a column, tried to peer down, on one side and the other, but no ray of light reached the ground: it might be a little drop of a couple of yards, or an abyss. The only thing he could do was continue advancing up where he was.

The avenue of escape was not long in appearing. It was a flat surface, a pale glimmer, next to the wall: perhaps the roof of a building, of cement – as Marcovaldo realized, when he began to walk on it – which extended into the darkness. He immediately regretted having ventured onto it; now he had lost all reference-points, he had moved away from the line of street-lights, and every step he took might bring him to the edge of the roof or, beyond it, into the void.

The void really was a chasm. From below little lights glowed, as if at a great distance, and if those were the street-lights down there, the ground must be much lower still. Marcovaldo found himself suspended in a space impossible to imagine: at times, up above, red and green lights appeared, arranged in irregular figures, like constellations. Peering at those lights, with his nose in the air, he soon took a step into the void and fell headlong.

"I'm dead!" he thought; but at the same moment he found himself seated on some soft earth; his hands touched some grass; he had fallen, unharmed, into the midst of a meadow. The low lights, which had seemed so distant to him, were a line of little bulbs at ground-level.

A peculiar place to put lights, but convenient all the same, because they marked out a path for him. His foot now was not treading on grass but on asphalt: in the midst of the meadow a broad paved street passed, illuminated by those luminous beams at ground-level. Around him, nothing: only the very high, colored lights, which appeared and disappeared.

"A paved road is sure to lead somewhere," Marcovaldo thought, and started following it. He arrived at a fork, or rather, at an intersection, where every branch of the road was flanked by those little low bulbs and huge white numbers were marked on the ground.

He lost heart. What did it matter which direction he chose to follow if, all around, there was only this flat grassy meadow and this empty fog? It was at this point that he saw, at a man's height, a movement of beams of light. A man, really a man, with his arms open, dressed – it seemed – in a yellow overall, was waving two luminous little disks like the kind station-masters wave.

Marcovaldo ran towards this man and, even before reaching him, he started saying breathlessly: "Hey, hey, listen, here in the midst of the fog, how do I – "

"Don't worry," the voice of the man in yellow replied. "Above a thousand meters there's no fog, you can proceed safely. The steps are just ahead; the others have already boarded."

The words were obscure, but heartening: Marcovaldo

was particularly pleased to hear there were other people not far away; he advanced to join them, without asking further questions.

The mysteriously announced steps were a little stairway with comfortable steps and two railings, white in the darkness. Marcovaldo climbed up. On the threshold of a low doorway, a girl greeted him so cordially it seemed impossible she was actually addressing him.

Marcovaldo bowed and scraped. "My humble respects, Signorina." Steeped in cold and dampness as he was, he was dazed at finding refuge under a roof . . .

He entered, blinked, his eyes blinded by the light. He wasn't in a house. He was – where? In a bus, he thought, a long bus with many empty places. He sat down. As a rule, going home from work, he never took the bus, but chose the tram because the ticket cost a bit less. This time, however, he was lost in a neighborhood so remote that surely there was only a bus service. How lucky he was to have arrived in time to catch this one, no doubt the last! And what soft, comfortable seats! Marcovaldo, now that he had found out about it, would always take the bus, even if the passengers were obliged to obey some rules (". . . Please," a loudspeaker was saying, "refrain from smoking and fasten your seatbelts . . ."), even if the roar of the motor, as it started, was excessive.

A man in uniform passed among the seats. "Excuse me, conductor," Marcovaldo said. "Do you know if there's a stop anywhere near Via Pancrazio Pancrazietti?"

"What are you talking about, sir? Our first stop is Bombay, then we go on to Calcutta and Singapore."

Marcovaldo looked around. In the other places were seated impassive Indians, with beards and turbans. There were also a few women, wrapped in embroidered saris, a painted spot on their brow. The night beyond the windows was full of stars, now that the plane had passed through the thick blanket of fog, and was flying in the limpid sky of the great altitudes.

SPRING

13. Where the river is more blue?

It was a time when the simplest foods contained threats, traps, and frauds. Not a day went by without some newspaper telling of ghastly discoveries in the housewife's shopping: cheese was made of plastic, butter from tallow candles; in fruit and vegetables the arsenic of insecticides was concentrated in percentages higher than the vitamin content; to fatten chickens they stuffed them with synthetic pills that could transform the man who ate a drumstick into a chicken himself. Fresh fish had been caught the previous year in Iceland and they put make-up on the eyes to make it seem yesterday's catch. Mice had been found in several milk-bottles, whether dead or alive was not made clear. From the tins of oil it was no longer the golden juice of the olive that flowed, but the fat of old mules, cleverly distilled.

At work or in the café Marcovaldo heard them discussing these things, and every time he felt something like a mule's kick in his stomach, or a mouse running down his esophagus. At home, when his wife, Domitilla, came back from the market, the sight of her shopping-bag, which once had given him such joy with its celery and eggplant, the rough, absorbent paper of the packages from the grocer or the delicatessen, now filled him with fear, as if hostile presences had infiltrated the walls of his house.

"I must bend all my efforts," he vowed to himself,

"towards providing my family with food that hasn't passed through the treacherous hands of speculators." In the morning, going to work, he sometimes encountered men with fishing-poles and rubber boots, heading for the river. "That's the way," Marcovaldo said to himself. But the river, there in the city, which collected garbage and waste and the emptying of sewers, filled him with deep repugnance. "I have to look for a place," he said to himself, "where the water is really water, and fish are really fish. There I'll drop my line."

The days were growing longer: with his motorbike, after work, Marcovaldo set to exploring the river along its course before the city, and the little streams, its tributaries. He was specially interested in the stretches where the water flowed farthest from the paved road. He proceeded along paths, among the clumps of willows, riding his motorbike as far as he could go, then – after leaving it in a bush – on foot, until he reached the stream. Once he got lost: he roamed among steep, overgrown slopes, and could find no trail, nor did he know in which direction the river lay. Then, all of a sudden, pushing some branches aside, he saw the silent water a few feet below him – it was a widening of the river, practically a calm little pool – of such a blue that it seemed a mountain lake.

His emotion didn't prevent him from peering down among the little ripples of the stream. And there, his stubbornness was rewarded! A flicker, the unmistakable flash of a fin at the surface, and then another, another still: such happiness, he could hardly believe his eyes. This was the place where the fish of the whole river assembled, the fisherman's paradise, perhaps still unknown to everyone but him. On his way home (it was already growing dark) he stopped and cut signs on the bark of the elms, and made piles of stones at certain spots, to be able to find the way again.

Now he had only to equip himself. Actually, he had already thought about it: among the neighbors and the personnel of his firm he had already identified about ten dedicated fishermen. With hints and allusions, promising each to inform him, the moment he was really sure, of a place full of tench that only he knew about, he managed to borrow, a bit from one, a bit from another, the most complete fisherman's outfit ever seen.

Now he lacked nothing: pole, line, hooks, bait, net, boots, creel. One fine morning, in a couple of hours – from six to eight, before going to work, at the river with the tench – could he fail to catch some? And in fact, he had only to drop his line and he caught them; the tench bit, without any suspicion. Since it was so easy with hook and line, he tried with the net; the tench were so good-natured that they rushed headlong into the net, too.

When it was time to leave, his creel was already full. He looked for a path, moving up the river.

"Hey, you!" At a curve in the shore, among the poplars, there was a character wearing a guard's cap, and giving him an ugly stare.

"Me? What is it?" Marcovaldo asked, sensing an unknown threat to his tench.

"Where did you catch those fish there?" the guard asked.

"Eh? Why?" And Marcovaldo's heart was already in his mouth.

"If you caught them down below, throw them back right now: didn't you see the factory up there?" And the man pointed out a long, low building that now, having come around the bend of the river, Marcovaldo could discern, beyond the willows, throwing smoke into the air and, into the water, a dense cloud of an incredible color somewhere between turquoise and violet. "You must at least have seen the color of the water! A paint factory: the river's poisoned because of that blue, and the fish are poisoned, as well. Throw them back right now, or I'll confiscate them!"

Marcovaldo would have liked to fling them far away as fast as possible, get rid of them, as if the mere smell were enough to poison him. But in front of the guard, he didn't want to humble himself. "What if I caught them farther up?"

"Then that's another story. I'll confiscate them and fine you, too. Above the factory there's a fishing preserve. Can't you see the sign?"

"Actually," Marcovaldo hastened to say, "I carry a fishing-pole just for looks, to fool my friends. I really bought the fish at the village shop nearby."

"Then everything's all right. You only have to pay the tax, to take them into the city: we're beyond the city limits here."

Marcovaldo had already opened the creel and was emptying it into the river. Some of the tench must have been still alive, because they darted off with great joy.

SUMMER

14. Moon and GNAC

The night lasted twenty seconds, then came twenty seconds of GNAC. For twenty seconds you could see the blue sky streaked with black clouds, the gilded sickle of the waxing moon, outlined by an impalpable halo, and stars that, the more you looked at them, the denser their poignant smallness became, to the sprinkle of the Milky Way: all this seen in great haste; every detail you dwelt on was something of the whole that you lost, because the twenty seconds quickly ended and the GNAC took over.

The GNAC was a part of the neon sign SPAAK-COGNAC on the roof opposite, which shone for twenty seconds then went off for twenty, and when it was lighted you couldn't see anything else. The moon suddenly faded, the sky became a flat, uniform black, the stars lost their radiance, and the cats, male and female, that for ten seconds had been letting out howls of love, moving languidly towards each other along the drainpipes and the roof-trees, squatted on the tiles, their fur bristling in the phosphorescent neon light.

Leaning out of the attic where they lived, Marcovaldo's family was traversed by conflicting trains of thought. It was night, and Isolina, a big girl by now, felt carried away by the moonlight; her heart yearned, and even the faintest croaking of a radio from the lower floors of the building came to her like the notes of a serenade; there was the GNAC, and that radio seemed to take on a different rhythm, a jazz beat, and Isolina thought of the dance-hall full of blazing lights and herself, poor thing, up here all alone. Pietruccio and Michelino stared wide-eyed into the night and let themselves be invaded by a warm, soft fear of being surrounded by forests full of brigands; then, GNAC!, and they sprang up with thumbs erect and forefingers extended, one against the other: "Hands up! I'm the Lone Ranger!" Domitilla, their mother, every time the light was turned off, thought: "Now the children must be sent to bed; this air could be bad for them; and Isolina shouldn't be looking out of the window at this hour: it's not proper!" But then everything was again luminous, electric, outside and inside, and Domitilla felt as if she were paying a visit to the home of someone important.

Fiordaligi, on the contrary, a melancholy youth, every time the GNAC went off, saw the dimly lighted window of a garret appear behind the curl of the G, and beyond the pane the face of a moon-colored girl, neon-colored, the color of light in the night, a mouth still almost a child's that, the moment he smiled at her, parted imperceptibly and seemed almost to open in a smile; then all of a sudden from the darkness that implacable G of GNAC burst out again, and the face lost its outline, was transformed into a weak, pale shadow, and he could no longer tell if the girlish mouth had responded to his smile.

In the midst of this storm of passions, Marcovaldo was trying to teach his children the positions of the celestial bodies.

"That's the Great Bear: one, two, three, four, and there, the tail. And that's the Little Bear. And the Pole-Star that means North."

"What does that one over there mean?"

"It means C. But that doesn't have anything to do with the stars. It's the last letter of the word COGNAC. The stars mark the four cardinal points. North South East West. The moon's hump is to the west. Hump to the west, waxing moon. Hump to the east, waning moon."

"Is cognac waning, Papà? The *C*'s hump is to the east!"

"Waxing and waning have nothing to do with that: it's a sign the Spaak company has put there."

"What company put up the moon then?"

"The moon wasn't put up by a company. It's a satellite, and it's always there."

"If it's always there, why does it keep changing its hump?"

"It's the quarters. You only see a part of it."

"You only see a part of COGNAC too."

"Because the roof of the Pierbernardi building is higher."

"Higher than the moon?"

And so, every time the GNAC came on, Marcovaldo's stars became mixed up with terrestrial commerce, and Isolina transformed a sigh into a low humming of a mambo, and the girl of the garret disappeared in that cold and dazzling arc, hiding her response to the kiss that Fiordaligi had finally summoned the courage to blow her on his fingertips, and Filippetto and Michelino, their fists to their faces, played at strafing: Tat–tat–tat–tat . . . against the glowing sign, which, after its twenty seconds, went off.

"Tat–tat–tat . . . Did you see that, Papà? I shot it out with just one burst." Filippetto said, but already, outside the neon light, his warlike mania had vanished and his eyes were filling with sleep.

"If you only had!" his father blurted. "If it had only been blown to bits! I'd show you Leo the lion, the Twins . . ."

"Leo the lion!" Michelino was overcome with enthusiasm. "Wait!" He had an idea. He took his slingshot, loaded it with gravel, of which he always carried a reserve pocketful, and fired a volley of pebbles, with all his strength, at the GNAC.

They heard the shower fall, scattered, on the tiles of the roof opposite, on the tin of the drainpipes, the tinkle at the panes of a window that had been struck, the gong of a pebble plunging down on the metal shield of a street-light, a voice from below: "It's raining stones! Hey, you up there! Hoodlum." But at the very moment of the shooting the neon sign had turned off at the end of its twenty seconds. And everyone in the attic room began counting mentally: one two three, ten eleven, up to twenty. They counted nineteen, held their breath, they counted twenty, they counted twenty-one twenty-two, for fear of having counted too fast. But no, not at all: the GNAC didn't come on again; it remained a black curlicue, hard to decipher, twined around its scaffolding like a vine around a pergola. "Aaaah!" they all shouted and the hood of the sky rose, infinitely starry, above them.

Marcovaldo, his hand frozen halfway towards the slap he meant to give Michelino, felt as if he had been flung into space. The darkness that now reigned at roof-level made a kind of obscure barrier that shut out the world below, where yellow and green and red hieroglyphics continued to whirl, and the winking eyes of traffic-lights, and the luminous navigation of empty trams, and the invisible cars that cast in front of them the bright cone of their headlights. From this world only a diffuse phosphorescence rose up this high, vague as smoke. And raising your eyes, no longer blinded, you saw the perspective of space unfold, the constellations expanded in depth, the firmament turning in every direction, a sphere that contains everything and is contained by no boundary, and only a thinning of its weft, like a breach, opened towards Venus, to make it stand out alone over the frame of the earth, with its steady slash of light exploded and concentrated at one point.

Suspended in this sky, the new moon – rather than display the abstract appearance of a half-moon – revealed its true nature as an opaque sphere, its whole outline illuminated by the oblique rays of a sun the earth had lost, though it retained (as you can see only on certain early-summer nights) its warm color. And Marcovaldo, looking at that narrow shore of moon cut there between shadow and light, felt a nostalgia, as if yearning to arrive at a beach which had stayed miraculously sunny in the night.

And so they remained at the window of the garret, the children frightened by the measureless consequences of their act, Isolina carried away as if in ecstasy, Fiordaligi, who, alone among all, discerned the dimly lighted garret and finally the girl's lunar smile. Their Mamma recovered herself: "Come on now, it's night. What are you doing at the window? You'll catch something, in this moonlight!"

Michelino aimed his slingshot up high. "Now I'll turn off the moon!" He was seized and put to bed.

And so for the rest of that night and all through the night following, the neon sign on the other roof said only SPAAK-CO, and from Marcovaldo's garret you could see the firmament. Fiordaligi and the lunar girl blew each other kisses, and perhaps, speaking to each other in sign language, they would manage to make a date to meet.

But on the morning of the second day, on the roof, in the scaffolding that supported the neon sign, the tiny forms of two electricians in overalls were visible, as they checked the tubes and wires. With the air of old men who predict changes in the weather, Marcovaldo stuck his head out and said: "Tonight there'll be GNAC again."

Somebody knocked at the garret. They opened the door. It was a gentleman wearing eyeglasses. "I beg your pardon, could I take a look at your window? Thanks." And he introduced himself: "Godifredo, neon advertising agent."

"We're ruined! They want us to pay the damages!" Marcovaldo thought, and he was already devouring his children with his eyes, forgetting his astronomical transports. "Now he'll look at the window and realize the stones could only have come from here." He tried to ward this off. "You know how it is, the kids shoot at the sparrows. Pebbles. I don't know how that Spaak sign went out. But I punished them, all right. Oh yes indeed, I punished them! And you can be sure it won't happen again."

Signor Godifredo's face became alert. "Actually, I'm

employed by 'Tomahawk Cognac', not by Spaak. I had
come to examine the possibility of a sign on this roof. But
do go on: I'm interested in what you're saying."

And so it was that Marcovaldo, half an hour later, concluded a deal with Tomahawk Cognac, Spaak's chief rival.
The children should empty their slingshots at the GNAC
every time the sign was turned on again.

"That should be the straw that will break the camel's
back," Signor Godifredo said. He was not mistaken: already
on the verge of bankruptcy because of its large advertising
outlay, Spaak and Co. took the constant damaging of its
most beautiful neon signs as a bad omen. The sign that now
sometimes said COGAC and sometimes CONAC or
CONC spread among the firm's creditors the impression of
financial difficulties; at a certain point, the advertising agency
refused to make further repairs if arrears were not paid; the
turned-off sign increased the alarm among the creditors;
and Spaak went out of business.

In the sky of Marcovaldo the full moon shone, round, in
all its splendor.

It was in the last quarter when the electricians came back
to clamber over the roof opposite. And that night, in letters
of fire, letters twice as high and broad as before, they could
read TOMAHAWK COGNAC, and there was no longer
moon or firmament or sky or night, only TOMAHAWK
COGNAC, TOMAHAWK COGNAC, TOMAHAWK
COGNAC, which blinked on and off every two seconds.

The worst hit was Fiordaligi; the garret of the lunar girl
had vanished behind an enormous, impenetrable *W*.

AUTUMN

15. The rain and the leaves

At his job, among his various other responsibilities, Marcovaldo had to water every morning the potted plant in the entrance hall. It was one of those green house-plants with an erect, thin stalk from which, on both sides, broad, long-stemmed, shiny leaves stick out: in other words, one of those plants that are so plant-shaped, with leaves so leaf-shaped, that they don't seem real. But still it was a plant, and as such it suffered, because staying there, between the curtain and the umbrella-stand, it lacked light, air, and dew. Every morning Marcovaldo discovered some nasty sign: the stem of one leaf drooped as if it could no longer support the weight, another leaf was becoming spotted like the cheek of a child with measles, the tip of a third leaf was turning yellow; until, one or the other, plop!, was found on the floor. Meanwhile (what most wrung his heart) the plant's stalk grew taller, taller, no longer making orderly fronds, but naked as a pole, with a clump at the top that made it resemble a palm-tree.

Marcovaldo cleared away the fallen leaves, dusted the healthy ones, poured at the foot of the plant (slowly, so the pot wouldn't spill over and dirty the tiles) half a watering-can of water, immediately absorbed by the earth in the pot. And to these simple actions he devoted an attention he gave no other task of his, almost like the compassion felt for the

77

troubles of a relative. And he sighed, whether for the plant or himself: because in that lanky, yellowing bush within the company walls he recognized a companion in misfortune.

The plant (this was how it was called, simply, as if any more specific name were useless in a setting where it alone had to represent the vegetable kingdom) had become such a part of Marcovaldo's life that it dominated his thoughts at every hour of the day and night. When he examined the gathering clouds in the sky, his gaze now was no longer that of a city-dweller, wondering whether or not he should wear his raincoat, but that of a farmer expecting from day to day the end of a drought. And the moment when he raised his head from his work and saw, against the light, beyond the little window of the warehouse, the curtain of rain that had begun to fall, thick and silent, he would drop everything, run to the plant, take the pot in his arms, and set it outside in the courtyard.

The plant, feeling the water run over its leaves, seemed to expand, to offer the greatest possible surface to the drops, and in its joy it seemed to don its most brilliant green: or at least so Marcovaldo thought, as he lingered to observe it, forgetting to take shelter.

They stayed there in the courtyard, man and plant, facing each other, the man almost feeling plant-sensations under the rain, the plant – no longer accustomed to the open air and to the phenomena of nature – amazed, much like a man who finds himself suddenly drenched from head to foot, his clothes soaked. Marcovaldo, his nose in the air, sniffed the smell of the rain, a smell – for him – already of woods and fields, and he pursued with his mind some vague memories. But among these memories there surfaced, clearer and closer, that of the rheumatic aches that afflicted him every year; and then, hastily, he went back inside.

When working hours were over, the place had to be locked up. Marcovaldo asked the warehouse foreman: "Can I leave the plant outside there, in the courtyard?"

The foreman, Signor Viligelmo, was the kind of man

who avoided burdensome responsibilities: "Are you crazy? What if somebody steals it? Who'll answer for that?"

But Marcovaldo, seeing how much good the rain did the plant, couldn't bring himself to put it back inside: it would mean wasting that gift of heaven. "I could keep it until tomorrow morning . . ." he suggested. "I'll load it on the rack of my bike and take it home . . . That way it'll get as much rain as possible."

Signor Viligelmo thought it over a moment, then concluded: "Then you're taking the responsibility." And he gave his consent.

Under the pouring rain, Marcovaldo crossed the city, bent over the handle-bars of his motorbike, bundled up in a rain-proof wind-breaker. Behind him, on the rack, he had tied the pot; and bike, man, and plant seemed a sole thing; indeed the hunched and bundled man disappeared, and you saw only a plant on a bicycle. Every now and then, from beneath his hood, Marcovaldo looked around until he could see a dripping leaf flapping behind him: and every time it seemed to him that the plant had become taller and more leafy.

At home, a garret with its window-sill on the roof, the moment Marcovaldo arrived with the pot in his arms, the children started dancing around it.

"The Christmas tree! The Christmas tree!"

"No, no, what are you talking about? Christmas is a long way off yet!" Marcovaldo protested. "Watch out for those leaves, they're delicate!"

"We're already like sardines in a can, in this house," Domitilla grumbled. "If you bring a tree in, too, we'll have to move out . . ."

"It's only a plant! I'll put it on the window-sill . . ."

The shadowy form of the plant on the sill could be seen from the room. Marcovaldo, at supper, didn't look at his plate, but beyond the window-panes.

Ever since they had left the half-basement for the garret, the life of Marcovaldo and family had greatly improved.

However, living up under the roof also had its drawbacks: the ceiling, for example, leaked a little. The drops fell in four or five distinct places, at regular intervals; and Marcovaldo put basins under them, or pots. On rainy nights when all of them were in bed, they could hear the tic-toc-tuc of the various drips, which made him shudder as if at a premonition of rheumatism. That night, on the contrary, every time Marcovaldo woke from his restless sleep and pricked up his ears, the tic-toc-tuc seemed cheery music to him: it told him the rain was continuing, mild and steady, and was nourishing the plant, driving the sap up along its delicate stalks, unfolding the leaves like sails. Tomorrow, when I look out, I'll find it has grown! he thought.

But even though he had thought about this, when he opened the window in the morning, he couldn't believe his eyes: the plant now filled half the window, the leaves had at least doubled in number, and no longer drooped under their own weight, but were erect and sharp as swords. He climbed down the steps, with the pot clutched to him, tied it to the rack, and rushed to work.

The rain had stopped, but the weather was still uncertain. Marcovaldo hadn't even climbed out of his seat when a few drops started falling again. "Since the rain does it so much good, I'll leave it in the courtyard again," he thought.

In the warehouse, every now and then he went to peek out of the window onto the courtyard. His distraction from work did not please the foreman. "Well, what's wrong with you this morning? Always looking out of the window."

"It's growing! Come and see for yourself, Signor Viligelmo!" And Marcovaldo motioned to him, speaking almost in a whisper, as if the plant were not to overhear. "Look how it's growing! It really has grown, hasn't it?"

"Yes, it's grown quite a bit," the boss conceded, and for Marcovaldo this was one of those satisfactions that life on the job rarely grants the personnel.

It was Saturday. Work ended at one and they were all off until Monday. Marcovaldo would have liked to take the plant home with him again, but now, since it was no longer raining, he couldn't think of any pretext. The sky, however, was not clear: black cumulus clouds were scattered here and there. He went to the foreman, who, a meteorology enthusiast, kept a barometer hanging over his desk. "What's the forecast, Signor Viligelmo?"

"Bad, still bad," he said. "For that matter, though it's not raining here, it is in the neighborhood where I live. I just telephoned my wife."

"In that case," Marcovaldo quickly proposed, "I'll take the plant on a little trip where it's raining," and, no sooner said than done, he fixed the pot again on the rack of his bike.

Saturday afternoon and Sunday Marcovaldo spent in this fashion: bouncing on the seat of his motorbike, the plant behind him, he studied the sky, seeking a cloud that seemed in the right mood, then he would race through the streets until he encountered rain. From time to time, turning around, he saw the plant a bit taller: high as the taxis, as the delivery trucks, as the trams! And with broader and broader leaves, from which the rain slid onto his rain-proof hood like a shower.

By now it was a tree on two wheels, speeding through the city, bewildering traffic cops, drivers, pedestrians. And the clouds, at the same time, sped along the paths of the wind, spattering a neighborhood with rain, then abandoning it; and the passers-by, one after another, stuck out their hands and closed their umbrellas; and along streets and avenues and squares, Marcovaldo chased his cloud, bent over his handle-bars, bundled in his hood from which only his nose protruded, his little motor putt-putting along at full tilt, as he kept the plant in the trajectory of the drops, as if the trail of rain that the cloud drew after itself had got caught in the leaves and thus all rushed ahead, drawn by the same power: wind, cloud, rain, plant, wheels.

On Monday Marcovaldo presented himself, empty-handed, to Signor Viligelmo.

"Where's the plant?" the foreman asked at once.

"Outside. Come."

"Where?" Viligelmo said. "I don't see it."

"It's that one over there. It's grown a bit . . ." and he pointed to a tree that reached the third floor. It was no longer planted in its old pot but in a kind of barrel, and instead of using his bike Marcovaldo had had to borrow a little motor-truck.

"Now what?" The boss was infuriated. "How can we get it into the entrance hall? It won't go through the doors any more!"

Marcovaldo shrugged.

"The only thing," Viligelmo said, "is to give it back to the nursery, in exchange for a plant of the right size!"

Marcovaldo climbed onto his bike again. "I'll go."

He resumed his dash through the city. The tree filled the center of the streets with green. The cops, concerned about traffic, stopped him at every intersection; then – when Marcovaldo explained that he was taking the plant back to the nursery, to get rid of it – they let him go on. But, taking first this street then that, Marcovaldo couldn't bring himself to turn into the one to the nursery. He hadn't the heart to give up his creature, now that he had raised it with such success: nothing in his whole life, it seemed to him, had given him the satisfaction he had received from that plant.

And so he went on, to and fro among streets and squares and embankments and bridges. And foliage worthy of a tropical forest spread out until it covered his head, back, arms, until he had disappeared into the green. And all these leaves and stems of leaves and the stalk, too (which had remained very slim), swayed and swayed as if in a constant trembling, whether a downpour of rain was still striking them, or whether the drops became rarer or stopped altogether.

The rain ceased. It was the hour towards sunset. At the end of the streets, in the space between the houses, a light mixed with rainbow settled. The plant, after that impetuous effort of growth that had involved it as long as the rain lasted, was virtually exhausted. Continuing his aimless race, Marcovaldo didn't notice that, behind him, the intense green of the leaves, one by one, was turning to yellow, a golden yellow.

For quite a while already, a procession of motorbikes and cars and bicycles and children had been following the tree that was moving about the city, without Marcovaldo's becoming aware of them, and they were shouting: "The baobab! The babobab!" and with great "Ooooh's!" of wonder they watched the yellowing of the leaves. When one leaf dropped and flew off, many hands were raised to catch it in flight.

A wind sprang up; the golden leaves, in gusts, darted off in midair, spinning. Marcovaldo still thought that, behind him, he had the green, thick tree, when all of a sudden – perhaps feeling himself unsheltered in the wind – he looked back. The tree was gone: there was only a thin stick, from which extended a monstrance of bare stems, and one last yellow leaf at the top still. In the light of the rainbow everything else seemed black: the people on the sidewalks, the façades of the houses that served as backdrop; and over this black, in midair, the golden leaves twirled, shining, hundreds of them; and hundreds of hands, red and pink, rose from the darkness to grab them; and the wind lifted the golden leaves towards the rainbow there at the end of the street, and the hands, and the shouts; and it detached even the last leaf, which turned from yellow to orange, then red, violet, blue, green, then yellow again, and then vanished.

WINTER

16. *Marcovaldo at the supermarket*

At six in the evening the city fell into the hands of the consumers. All during the day the big occupation of the productive public was to produce: they produced consumer goods. At a certain hour, as if a switch had been thrown, they stopped production and, away!, they were all off, to consume. Every day an impetuous flowering barely had time to blossom inside the lighted shop-windows, the red salamis to hang, the towers of porcelain dishes to rise to the ceiling, the rolls of fabric to unfurl folds like peacock's tails, when lo! the consuming throng burst in, to dismantle, to gnaw, to grope, to plunder. An uninterrupted line wound along all the sidewalks and under the arcades, extended through the glass doors of the shops to all the counters, nudged onwards by each individual's elbows in the ribs of the next, like the steady throb of pistons. Consume! And they touched the goods and put them back and picked them up again and tore them from one another's hands; consume! and they forced the pale salesladies to display on the counter linen and more linen; consume! and the spools of colored string spun like tops, the sheets of flowered paper fluttered their wings, enfolding purchases in little packages, and the little packages in big packages, bound, each, with its butter-fly knot. And off went packages and bundles and wallets and bags; they whirled around the cashier's desk in a clutter, hands digging into pocketbooks seeking change-purses, and fingers rummaging in change-purses for coins, and down below, in a forest of alien legs and hems of overcoats, children no longer held by the hand became lost and started crying.

One of these evenings Marcovaldo was taking his family out for a walk. Since they had no money, their entertainment was to watch others go shopping; for the more money circulates, the more those without any can hope — sooner or later a bit of it will come into my pockets. But, on the contrary, Marcovaldo's wages, because they were scant and the family was large, and there were instalments and debts to be paid, flowed away the moment he collected them. Anyhow, watching was always lovely, especially if you took a turn around the supermarket.

This was a self-service supermarket. It provided those carts, like iron baskets on wheels; and each customer pushed his cart along, filling it with every sort of delicacy. Marcovaldo, on entering, also took a cart; his wife, another; and his four children took one each. And so they marched in procession, their carts before them, among counters piled high with mountains of good things to eat, pointing out to one another the salamis and the cheeses, naming them, as if in a crowd they had recognized the faces of friends, or acquaintances, anyway.

"Papà, can we take this, at least?" the children asked every minute.

"No, hands off! Mustn't touch," Marcovaldo said, remembering that, at the end of this stroll, the check-out girl was waiting, to total up the sum.

"Then why is that lady taking one?" they insisted, seeing all these good housewives who, having come in to buy only a few carrots and a bunch of celery, couldn't resist the sight of a pyramid of jars and plonk plonk plonk! with a partly absent and partly resigned movement, they sent cans of tomatoes, peaches, anchovies, thudding into their carts.

In other words, if your cart is empty and the others are

full, you can hold out only so long: then you're over-
whelmed by envy, heartbreak, and you can't stand it. So
Marcovaldo, having told his wife and children not to touch
anything, made a rapid turn at one of the intersections,
eluded his family's gaze, and, having taken a box of dates
from a shelf, put it in his cart. He wanted only to experience
the pleasure of pushing it around for ten minutes, displaying
his purchases like everyone else, and then replace it where he
had taken it. This box, plus a red bottle of ketchup and a
package of coffee and a blue pack of spaghetti. Marcovaldo
was sure that, restraining himself for at least a quarter of an
hour, and without spending a cent, he could savor the joy of
those who know how to choose the product. But if the
children were to see him, that would spell trouble! They
would immediately start imitating him and God only knows
the confusion that would lead to!

Marcovaldo tried to cover his tracks, moving along a
zig-zag course through the departments, now following
busy maidservants, now be-furred ladies. And as one or the
other extended her hand to select a fragrant yellow squash
or a box of triangular processed cheeses, he would imitate
her. The loudspeakers were broadcasting gay little tunes:
the consumers moved or paused, following the rhythm,
and at the right moment they stretched out their arms,
picked up an object and set it in their baskets, all to the sound
of music.

Marcovaldo's cart was now filled with merchandise; his
footsteps led him into the less frequented departments,
where products with more and more undecipherable names
were sealed in boxes with pictures from which it was not
clear whether these were fertilizer for lettuce or lettuce
seeds or actual lettuce or poison for lettuce-caterpillars or
feed to attract the birds that eat those caterpillars or else
seasoning for lettuce or for the roasted birds. In any case,
Marcovaldo took two or three boxes.

And so he was proceeding between two high hedges of
shelves. All at once the aisle ended and there was a long

space, empty and deserted, with neon lights that made the tiles gleam. Marcovaldo was there, alone with his cart full of things, and at the end of that empty space there was the exit with the cash-desk.

His first instinct was to break into a run, head down, pushing the cart before him like a tank, to escape from the supermarket with his booty before the check-out girl could give the alarm. But at that moment, from a nearby aisle, another cart appeared, even more loaded than his, and the person pushing it was his wife, Domitilla. And from somewhere else, yet another emerged, and Filippetto was pushing it with all his strength. At this area the aisles of many departments converged, and from each opening one of Marcovaldo's children appeared, all pushing carts laden like freighters. Each had had the same idea, and now, meeting, they realized they had assembled a complete sampling of all the supermarket's possibilities. "Papà, are we rich then?" Michelino asked. "Will we have food to eat for a year?"

"Go back! Hurry! Get away from the desk!" Marcovaldo cried, doing an about-face and hiding, himself and his victuals, behind the counters; and he began to dash, bent double as if under enemy fire, to become lost once more among the various departments. A rumble resounded behind him; he turned and saw the whole family, galloping at his heels, pushing their carts in line, like a train.

"They'll charge us a million for this!"

The supermarket was large and complex as a labyrinth: you could roam around it for hours and hours. With all these provisions at their disposal, Marcovaldo and family could have spent the winter there, never coming out. But the loudspeakers had already stopped their tunes, and were saying: "Attention, please! In fifteen minutes the supermarket will close! Please proceed to the check-out counters!"

It was time to get rid of their cargo: now or never. At the summons of the loudspeaker, the crowd of customers was gripped by a frantic haste, as if these were the last minutes in the last supermarket of the whole world, an urgency either to grab everything there was or to leave it there – the motive wasn't clear – and there was a pushing and shoving around all the shelves. Marcovaldo, Domitilla and the children took advantage of it to replace goods on the counters or to slip things into other people's carts. The replacements were somewhat random: the flypaper ended on the ham shelf, a cabbage landed among the cakes. They didn't realise that, instead of a cart, one lady was pushing a baby carriage with an infant inside: they stuck a bottle of Barbera in with it.

Depriving themselves of things like this, without even having tasted them, was a torment that brought tears to the eyes. And so, at the very moment they abandoned a jar of mayonnaise, they came upon a bunch of bananas, and took it; or a roast chicken to substitute for a nylon broom; with this system the more they emptied their carts, the more they filled them.

The family with their provisions went up and down the escalators, and at every level, on all sides they found themselves facing obligatory routes that led to a check-out cashier, who aimed an adding machine, chattering like a machine gun, at all those who showed signs of leaving. The wandering of Marcovaldo and family resembled more and more that of caged animals or of prisoners in a luminous prison with walls of colored panels.

In one place, the panels of one wall had been dismantled; there was a ladder set there, hammers, carpenter's and mason's tools. A contractor was building an annex to the supermarket. Their working day over, the men had gone off, leaving everything where it was. Marcovaldo, his provisions before him, passed through the hole in the wall. Ahead there was darkness: he advanced. And his family, with their carts, came after him.

The rubber wheels of the carts jolted over the ground, sandy at times, as if cobbles had been removed, then on a floor of loose planks. Marcovaldo proceeded, poised, along a plank; the others followed him. All of a sudden they saw, before and behind, above and below, many lights strewn in the darkness, and all around, the void.

They were on the wooden structure of a scaffolding, at the level of seven-storey houses. The city opened below them in a luminous sparkle of windows and signs and the electric spray from tram antennae; higher up, the sky was dotted with stars and red lights of radio stations' antennae. The scaffolding shook under the weight of all those goods teetering up there. Michelino said: "I'm scared!"

From the darkness a shadow advanced. It was an enormous mouth, toothless, that opened, stretching forward on a long metal neck: a crane. It descended on them, stopped at their level, the lower jaw against the edge of the scaffolding. Marcovaldo tilted the cart, emptied the goods into the iron maw, and moved forward. Domitilla did the same. The children imitated their parents. The crane closed its jaws, with all the supermarket loot inside, and, pulley creaking, drew back its neck and moved away. Below, the multicolored neon signs glowed and turned, inviting everyone to buy the products on sale in the great supermarket.

SPRING

17. Smoke, wind, and soap-bubbles

Every day the postman left some envelopes in the tenants'
boxes; only in Marcovaldo's there was never anything,
because nobody ever wrote him, and if it hadn't been for an
occasional dun from the light or the gas company, his box
would have been absolutely useless.

"Papà! There's mail!" Michelino shouted.

"Come off it!" he answered. "The same old ads!"

From all the letter-boxes a blue-and-yellow folded sheet
was protruding. It said that to achieve really good suds,
Blancasol was the best of products; anyone who presented
this blue-and-yellow paper would be given a free sample.

Since these sheets were narrow and long, some of them
jutted from the slot of the boxes; others lay on the ground,
crumpled, or only a bit mussed, because many tenants,
opening the box, would promptly throw away all the
advertising matter that crammed it. Filippetto, Pietruccio,
and Michelino, collecting some from the floor, slipping
some from the slots, and actually fishing others out with a
bit of wire, began to make a collection of Blancasol coupons.

"I have the most!"

"No! Count them! I have the most! You want to bet?"

Blancasol had conducted the advertising campaign
through the whole neighborhood, house to house. And
house to house, the young brothers started covering the

90

area, trying to corner the coupons. Some concierges drove them away, shouting: "You little crooks! What are you trying to steal? I'm going to call the police." Others were pleased to see the kids clean up some of the waste paper deposited there every day.

In the evening, Marcovaldo's two poor rooms were all blue and yellow with Blancasol ads; the children counted and recounted them and piled them into packs like bank tellers with banknotes.

"Papà, we have so many; couldn't we start a laundry?" Filippetto asked.

In those days, the detergent world was in great upheaval. Blancasol's advertising campaign had alarmed all the rival companies. To launch their products, they distributed through all the mailboxes of the city similar coupons, which entitled the recipient to larger and larger free samples.

Marcovaldo's children, in the days that followed, were kept very busy. Every morning the letter-boxes blossomed like peach-trees in spring: slips of paper with green drawings or pink, blue, orange, promised snow-white wash for those who used Washrite or Lavolux or Beautisuds or Handikleen. For the boys, the collecting of coupons and free-sample cards ramified into more and more new classifications. At the same time, their collection territory expanded, extending to the buildings on other streets.

Naturally, these maneuvers could not go unnoticed. The neighborhood kids soon realized what Michelino and his brothers went out hunting for all day, and immediately those papers, to which none of them had paid any attention before, became a sought-after booty. There was a period of rivalry among the various bands of kids, when the collection in one zone rather than another gave rise to disputes and brawling. Then, after a series of exchanges and negotiations, they reached an agreement: an organized system of hunting was more profitable than helter-skelter grabbing. And the collection of coupons became so methodical that the moment the man from Washrite or Rinsequik went by on his round of doorways, his route was observed and shadowed, step by step, and as fast as the material was distributed, it was confiscated by the kids.

Commanding operations, naturally, were still Filippetto, Pietruccio, and Michelino, because the idea had been theirs in the first place. They even succeeded in convincing the other boys that the coupons were common property and should be preserved all together. "Like in a bank!" Pietruccio explained.

"Do we own a laundry or a bank?" Michelino asked.

"Whatever it is, we're millionaires!"

The boys were so excited they couldn't sleep any more, and they made plans for the future.

"We only have to redeem all these samples and we'll have a huge amount of detergent."

"Where are we going to keep it?"

"We'll rent a warehouse!"

"Why not a freighter?"

Advertising, like fruits and flowers, has its seasons. After a few weeks, the detergent season ended; in the letter-boxes you found only ads for corn-removers.

"Shall we start collecting these, too?" someone suggested. But the prevailing view was that they should devote themselves at once to the redemption of their accumulated wealth of detergents. It was merely a matter of going to the prescribed shops and making them give a sample for every coupon. But this new phase of their plan, apparently quite simple, proved to be much longer and more complicated than the first.

Operations had to be conducted in skirmishing order: one kid at a time in one shop at a time. They could present three or even four coupons at once, provided they were of different brands; and if the clerks wanted to give only one sample of one brand, they had to say: "My Mamma wants to try them all to see which one's best."

Things became difficult when, in many shops, they would give the free sample only to those who bought something;

never had Mammas seen their children so eager to run errands to the grocery.

In other words, the transformation of coupons into goods was dragging out and required supplementary expenses because errands with Mamma's money were few and the shops to be covered were many. To procure funds the only course was to initiate phase three of the plan, namely the sale of the detergent already redeemed.

They decided to sell it door to door, ringing bells: "Signora! Are you interested? Perfect wash!" and they would hold out the box of Rinsequik or the packet of Blancasol.

"Yes, yes, thanks. Give it here," some of them said, and the moment they had the sample, they would slam the door in the boy's face.

"Hey? Where's the money?" And they would hammer their fists on the door.

"Money? Isn't it free? Go home, you naughty kids!"

In that same period, in fact, men hired by the various brands were going from home to home, leaving free samples: this was a new advertising offensive undertaken by the whole detergent industry, since the coupon campaign had not proved fruitful.

Marcovaldo's house looked like the basement of a grocery store, full as it was of products by Beautisuds, Handikleen, Lavolux; but from all this quantity of merchandise not a cent could be squeezed; it was stuff that's given away, like the water of drinking-fountains.

Naturally, among the company representatives the rumor soon spread that some kids were making the same rounds, door to door, selling the very product their representatives were begging housewives to accept free. In the world of trade waves of pessimism are frequent: they began to report that they, who were giving the stuff away, were told by housewives that they didn't have any use for detergents, while the same women actually bought the products from those who demanded money. The planning offices of the various firms got together, market research specialists were consulted: the conclusion they reached was that such unfair competition could be carried out only by receivers of stolen goods. The police, after bringing formal charges against criminals unknown, began to patrol the neighborhood, hunting for thieves and the hiding-place of their loot.

In a moment the detergents became as dangerous as dynamite. Marcovaldo was afraid. "I won't have even an ounce of this powder in my house!" But they didn't know where to put it; nobody wanted it at home. It was decided that the children would go and throw all of it into the river.

It was before dawn; on the bridge a little cart arrived, drawn by Pietruccio and pushed by his brothers, laden with boxes of Washrite and Lavolux, then another similar cart drawn by Uguccione, the son of the concierge across the street, and then others, many others. In the center of the bridge they stopped, they allowed a cyclist to pass. After he had cast a curious glance behind him, they cried: "Go!" Michelino began hurling boxes into the river.

"Stupid! Can't you see they float?" Filippetto cried. "You have to empty the powder into the river, not dump the box!"

And from the boxes, opened one by one, a soft white cloud drifted down, rested on the current that seemed to absorb it, reappeared in a swarm of tiny bubbles, then seemed to sink. "That's the way!" And the kids began emptying pounds and pounds.

"Look! Over there!" Michelino shouted, and pointed farther downstream.

After the bridge there were the falls. Where the stream began its descent, the bubbles were no longer visible; they reappeared farther down, but now they had become huge bubbles that swelled and pushed one another upwards from below, a wave of suds that rose and became gigantic, already it was as high as the falls, a whitish foam like a barber's mug lathered by his shaving-brush. It was as if all those powders of rival brands had made a point of demonstrating their frothiness: and the river was brimming with suds at the piers, and the fishermen, who at the first light were already in the water wearing their hip-boots, pulled in their lines and ran off.

A little breeze stirred the morning air. A clump of bubbles broke from the water's surface, and flew off, lightly. It was dawn and the bubbles took on a pink hue. The children saw them go off, high over their heads, and cried: "Ooooo . . ."

The bubbles flew on, following the invisible tracks of the city's currents of air; they turned into the streets at roof-level, always avoiding bumps with cornices and drainpipes. Now the compactness of the bunch had dissolved: the bubbles, first one then another, had flown off on their own, and each following a route different because of altitude and speed and path; they wandered in mid-air. They had multiplied, it seemed; indeed, they really had, because the river continued spilling over with foam like a pan of milk on the stove. And the wind, the wind raised up froths and frills and clumps that stretched out into rainbow garlands (the rays of the oblique sun, having climbed over the roofs, had now taken possession of the city and the river), and invaded the sky above the wires and antennae.

Dark shadows of workers rushed to the factories on their chattering motorbikes and the blue-green swarm hovering over them followed as if each man were pulling behind him a bunch of balloons tied by a long string to his handle-bars.

It was some people on a tram who first took notice. "Look! Look! What's that up there?" The tram-driver stopped and got out: all the passengers got out and started looking into the sky, the bikes and motorbikes stopped and the cars and the news-vendors and the bakers and all the morning passers-by and among them Marcovaldo on his way to work, and all stuck their noses in the air, following the flight of the soap-bubbles.

"Surely it's not some atomic thing?" an old woman asked, and fear ran through the crowd, and one man, seeing a bubble about to light on him, ran off, yelling: "It's radio-active!"

But the bubbles continued to glisten, multi-hued and fragile and so light that one puff, whoosh, and they were gone; and soon, in the crowd, the alarm died as it had flared up. "Radioactive my foot! It's soap! Soap-bubbles like kids blow!" And a frantic gaiety seized them. "Look at that one! And that! And that!" because they saw some enormous ones, of incredible dimensions, flying over, and as these bubbles grazed each other, they merged, they became double and triple, and the sky, the roofs, the tall buildings, through these transparent cupolas, appeared in shapes and colors never seen before.

From their smoke-stacks the factories had begun belching forth black smoke, as they did every morning. And the swarms of bubbles encountered the smoke-clouds and the sky was divided between currents of black smoke and currents of rainbow foam, and in the eddying wind they seemed to fight, and for a moment, only one moment, it looked as if the tops of the smoke-stacks were conquered by the bubbles, but soon there was such a mixture – between the smoke that imprisoned the rainbow foam and the globes of soap that imprisoned a veil of grains of soot – that you couldn't understand anything. Until, at a certain point, after seeking and seeking in the sky, Marcovaldo couldn't see the bubbles any longer, but only smoke, smoke, smoke.

SUMMER

18. The city all to himself

For eleven months of the year the inhabitants loved their city and woe to anyone who cast aspersions: the skyscrapers, the cigarette machines, the wide-screen movie theaters, all undeniable sources of constant attraction. The only citizen to whom this feeling could not be attributed with certitude was Marcovaldo; but what he thought – first – was hard to know since he didn't have great powers of communication, and – second – it mattered so little that it made no difference.

At a certain point in the year, the month of August began. And then you witnessed a general change of feeling. Nobody loved the city any more: even the skyscrapers and the pedestrian subways and the car-parks, till yesterday so cherished, had become disagreeable and tiresome. The inhabitants wanted only to get away as quickly as possible: and so, filling trains and clogging superhighways, by the 15th of the month all of them were actually gone. Except one. Marcovaldo was the only inhabitant not to leave the city.

He would go out to take a walk downtown, in the morning. The streets opened before him, broad and endless, drained of cars and deserted; the façades of the buildings, a gray fence of lowered iron shutters and the countless slats of the blinds, were sealed, like ramparts. For the whole year Marcovaldo had dreamed of being able to use the streets as streets, that is, walking in the middle of them: now he could do it, and he could also cross on the red light, and jay-walk, and stop in the center of squares. But he realized that the pleasure didn't come so much from doing these unaccustomed things as from seeing a whole different world: streets like the floors of valleys, or dry river-beds, houses like blocks of steep mountains, or the walls of a cliff.

To be sure, you immediately noticed the absence of something: but not the line of parked cars, or the jam at the intersection, or the flow of the crowd at the entrance to the department store, or the clump of people waiting for the tram; what was missing to fill the empty spaces and bend the squared surfaces was, say, a flood due to the bursting of water mains or an invasion of roots of the trees along the avenue which would crack the asphalt. Marcovaldo's eyes peered around seeking the emergence of a different city, a city of bark and scales and clots and nerve-systems under the city of paint and tar and glass and stucco. And there, the building which he passed every day was revealed to him, in its reality, as a quarry of porous gray sandstone; the fence of a building-site was of pine-planks still fresh, with knots that looked like buds; on the sign of the big fabric shop rested a host of little moths, asleep.

You would have said that, the moment human beings had deserted the city, it had fallen prey to inhabitants hidden till yesterday, who now gained the upper hand. For a bit Marcovaldo's stroll followed the itinerary of a file of ants, then let itself be turned aside by the flight of a bewildered scarab beetle, then lingered to accompany the twisting progress of a caterpillar. It wasn't only animals that invaded the area: Marcovaldo discovered that at the newspaper kiosks, on the northern side, a fine layer of mold had formed, that the potted trees outside restaurants made an effort to thrust their leaves beyond the frame of shadow of the sidewalk. But did the city still exist? That agglomerate of synthetic matter that confined Marcovaldo's days now proved to be a mosaic of disparate stones, each quite distinct from the others to sight and touch, in its hardness and heat and consistency.

And so, forgetting the function of sidewalks and zebra-stripes, Marcovaldo was moving through the streets with a butterfly's zig-zag, when all of a sudden the radiator of a sports car going at eighty miles per hour missed his hip by a fraction of an inch. Half in fear and half because of the blast, Marcovaldo leaped up and fell back, stunned.

The car, with a great snarl, braked, almost spinning full circle. A group of young men, in shirt sleeves, jumped out. "Now they'll beat me up," Marcovaldo thought, "because I was walking in the middle of the street!"

The young men were armed with strange implements. "At last we've found him! At last!" they said, surrounding Marcovaldo. "Here he is then," said one of them, holding a silvery little stick to his mouth, "the only inhabitant left in the city on the mid-August holiday. Excuse me, sir, would you mind telling our viewers your impressions?" and he stuck the silvery stick under Marcovaldo's nose.

A dazzling glow exploded, it was hot as a furnace, and Marcovaldo was about to faint. They had trained spotlights on him, cameras, microphones. He stammered something: at every three syllables he uttered, the young man moved in, twisting the microphone towards himself. "Ah, so you mean to say that . . ." and he would go on talking for ten minutes.

To put it simply: they were interviewing him.

"Can I go now?"

"Of course. Thank you very much . . . Actually, if you have nothing else to do . . . and feel like earning a little something . . . would you mind staying here and lending us a hand?"

The whole square was topsy-turvy: trucks, sound-trucks, cameras with dollies, batteries, lamps, teams of men in overalls, trundling from one place to another, all sweating.

"Here she is! She's here! She's here!" From an open limousine a movie star got out.

"Come on, guys, we can start the fountain sequence!"

The director of the TV report *August Follies* began to issue orders for shooting the famous star diving into the main fountain of the city.

To Marcovaldo, the grip, they had given the job of shifting around the square the bank of floodlights on a heavy stand. The great square now buzzed with machinery and sizzling arc-lights, resounded to hammering on makeshift metal scaffoldings, shouted commands . . . To Marcovaldo's eyes, blinded and dazed, the everyday city had resumed the place of that other city, glimpsed for a moment, or perhaps only dreamed.

AUTUMN

19. The garden of stubborn cats

The city of cats and the city of men exist one inside the other, but they are not the same city. Few cats recall the time when there was no distinction: the streets and squares of men were also streets and squares of cats, and the lawns, courtyards, balconies, and fountains: you lived in a broad and various space. But for several generations now domestic felines have been prisoners of an uninhabitable city: the streets are uninterruptedly overrun by the mortal traffic of cat-crushing automobiles; in every square foot of terrain where once a garden extended or a vacant lot or the ruins of an old demolition, now condominiums loom up, welfare housing, brand-new skyscrapers; every entrance is crammed with parked cars; the courtyards, one by one, have been roofed by reinforced concrete and transformed into garages or movie houses or storerooms or workshops. And where a rolling plateau of low roofs once extended, copings, terraces, water tanks, balconies, skylights, corrugated-iron sheds, now one general superstructure rises wherever structures can rise; the intermediate differences in height, between the low ground of the street and the supernal heaven of the penthouses, disappear; the cat of a recent litter seeks in vain the itinerary of its fathers, the point from which to make the soft leap from balustrade to cornice to drainpipe, or for the quick climb on the roof-tiles.

But in this vertical city, in this compressed city where all voids tend to fill up and every block of cement tends to mingle with other blocks of cement, a kind of counter-city opens, a negative city, that consists of empty slices between wall and wall, of the minimal distances ordained by the building regulations between two constructions, between the rear of one construction and the rear of the next; it is a city of cavities, wells, air conduits, driveways, inner yards, accesses to basements, like a network of dry canals on a planet of stucco and tar, and it is through this network, grazing the walls, that the ancient cat population still scurries.

On occasion, to pass the time, Marcovaldo would follow a cat. It was during the work-break, between noon and three, when all the personnel except Marcovaldo went home to eat, and he – who brought his lunch in his bag – laid his place among the packing-cases in the warehouse, chewed his snack, smoked a half-cigar, and wandered around, alone and idle, waiting for work to resume. In those hours, a cat that peeped in at a window was always welcome company, and a guide for new explorations. He had made friends with a tabby, well-fed, a blue ribbon around its neck, surely living with some well-to-do family. This tabby shared with Marcovaldo the habit of an afternoon stroll right after lunch; and naturally a friendship sprang up.

Following his tabby friend, Marcovaldo had started looking at places as if through the round eyes of a cat and even if these places were the usual environs of his firm he saw them in a different light, as settings for cattish stories, with connections practicable only by light, velvety paws. Though from the outside the neighborhood seemed poor in cats, every day on his rounds Marcovaldo made the acquaintance of some new face, and a miau, a hiss, a stiffening of fur on an arched back was enough for him to sense ties and intrigues and rivalries among them. At those moments he thought he had already penetrated the secrecy of the felines' society: and then he felt himself scrutinized by pupils that became slits, under the surveillance of the antennae of taut whiskers, and all the cats around him sat impassive as sphinxes, the pink triangle of their noses convergent on the black triangles of their lips, and the only things that moved were the tips of the ears, with a vibrant jerk like radar. They reached the end of a narrow passage, between squalid blank walls; and, looking around, Marcovaldo saw that the cats that had led him this far had vanished, all of them together, no telling in which direction, even his tabby friend, and they had left him alone. Their realm had territories, ceremonies, customs that it was not yet granted to him to discover.

On the other hand, from the cat city there opened unsuspected peep-holes onto the city of men: and one day the same tabby led him to discover the great Biarritz Restaurant.

Anyone wishing to see the Biarritz Restaurant had only to assume the posture of a cat, that is, proceed on all fours. Cat and man, in this fashion, walked around a kind of dome, at whose foot some low, rectangular little windows opened. Following the tabby's example, Marcovaldo looked down. They were transoms through which the luxurious hall received air and light. To the sound of gypsy violins, partridges and quails swirled by on silver dishes balanced by the white-gloved fingers of waiters in tailcoats. Or, more precisely, above the partridges and quails the dishes whirled, and above the dishes the white gloves, and poised on the waiters' patent-leather shoes, the gleaming parquet floor, from which hung dwarf potted palms and tablecloths and crystal and buckets like bells with the champagne bottle for their clapper: everything was turned upsidedown because Marcovaldo, for fear of being seen, wouldn't stick his head inside the window and confined himself to looking at the reversed reflection of the room in the tilted pane.

But it was not so much the windows of the dining-room as those of the kitchens that interested the cat: looking through the former you saw, distant and somehow transfigured, what in the kitchens presented itself – quite concrete and within paw's reach – as a plucked bird or a fresh fish. And it was towards the kitchens, in fact, that the tabby wanted to lead Marcovaldo, either through a gesture of altruistic friendship or else because it counted on the man's help for one of its raids. Marcovaldo, however, was reluctant to leave his belvedere over the main room: first as he was fascinated by the luxury of the place, and then because something down there had riveted his attention. To such an extent that, overcoming his fear of being seen, he kept peeking in, with his head in the transom.

In the midst of the room, directly under that pane, there was a little glass fish-tank, a kind of aquarium, where some fat trout were swimming. A special customer approached, a man with a shiny bald pate, black suit, black beard. An old waiter in tailcoat followed him, carrying a little net as if he were going to catch butterflies. The gentleman in black looked at the trout with a grave, intent air; then he raised one hand and with a slow, solemn gesture singled out a fish. The waiter dipped the net into the tank, pursued the appointed trout, captured it, headed for the kitchens, holding out in front of him, like a lance, the net in which the fish wriggled. The gentleman in black, solemn as a magistrate who has handed down a capital sentence, went to take his seat and wait for the return of the trout, sautéed "à la meunière".

If I found a way to drop a line from up here and make one of those trout bite, Marcovaldo thought, I couldn't be accused of theft; at worst, of fishing in an unauthorized place. And ignoring the miaus that called him towards the kitchens, he went to collect his fishing tackle.

Nobody in the crowded dining-room of the Biarritz saw the long, fine line, armed with hook and bait, as it slowly dropped into the tank. The fish saw the bait, and flung themselves on it. In the fray one trout managed to bite the worm: and immediately it began to rise, rise, emerge from the water, a silvery flash, it darted up high, over the laid tables and the trolleys of hors d'oeuvres, over the blue flames of the crêpes Suzette, until it vanished into the heavens of the transom.

Marcovaldo had yanked the rod with the brisk snap of the expert fisherman, so the fish landed behind his back. The trout had barely touched the ground when the cat sprang. What little life the trout still had was lost between the tabby's teeth. Marcovaldo, who had abandoned his line at that moment to run and grab the fish, saw it snatched from under his nose, hook and all. He was quick to put one foot on the rod, but the snatch had been so strong that the rod was all the man had left, while the tabby ran off with the fish, pulling the line after it. Treacherous kitty! It had vanished.

But this time it wouldn't escape him: there was that long line trailing after him and showing the way he had taken. Though he had lost sight of the cat, Marcovaldo followed the end of the line: there it was, running along a wall; it climbed a parapet, wound through a doorway, was swallowed up by a basement . . . Marcovaldo, venturing into more and more cattish places, climbed roofs, straddled railings, always managed to catch a glimpse – perhaps only a second before it disappeared – of that moving trace that indicated the thief's path.

Now the line played out down a sidewalk, in the midst of the traffic, and Marcovaldo, running after it, almost managed to grab it. He flung himself down on his belly: there, he grabbed it! He managed to seize one end of the line before it slipped between the bars of a gate.

Beyond a half-rusted gate and two bits of wall buried under climbing plants, there was a little rank garden, with a small, abandoned-looking building at the far end of it. A carpet of dry leaves covered the path, and dry leaves lay everywhere under the boughs of the two plane-trees, forming actually some little mounds in the yard. A layer of leaves was yellowing in the green water of a pool. Enormous buildings rose all around, skyscrapers with thousands of windows, like so many eyes trained disapprovingly on that little square patch with two trees, a few tiles, and all those yellow leaves, surviving right in the middle of an area of great traffic.

And in this garden, perched on the capitals and balustrades, lying on the dry leaves of the flower-beds, climbing on the trunks of the trees or on the drainpipes, motionless on their four paws, their tails making a question-mark, seated to wash their faces, there were tiger cats, black cats, white cats, calico cats, tabbies, angoras, Persians, house cats and stray cats, perfumed cats and mangy cats. Marcovaldo realized he had finally reached the heart of the cats' realm, their secret island. And, in his emotion, he almost forgot his fish.

It had remained, that fish, hanging by the line from the branch of a tree, out of reach of the cats' leaps; it must have dropped from its kidnapper's mouth at some clumsy movement, perhaps as it was defended from the others, or perhaps displayed as an extraordinary prize. The line had got tangled, and Marcovaldo, tug as he would, couldn't manage to yank it loose. A furious battle had meanwhile been joined among the cats, to reach that unreachable fish, or rather, to win the right to try and reach it. Each wanted to prevent the others from leaping: they hurled themselves on one another, they tangled in mid-air, they rolled around clutching each other, and finally a general war broke out in a whirl of dry, crackling leaves.

After many futile yanks, Marcovaldo now felt the line was free, but he took care not to pull it: the trout would have fallen right in the midst of that infuriated scrimmage of felines.

It was at this moment that, from the top of the walls of the gardens, a strange rain began to fall: fish-bones, heads, tails, even bits of lung and lights. Immediately the cats' attention was distracted from the suspended trout and they flung themselves on the new delicacies. To Marcovaldo, this seemed the right moment to pull the line and regain his fish. But, before he had time to act, from a blind of the little villa, two yellow, skinny hands darted out: one was brandishing scissors; the other, a frying-pan. The hand with the scissors was raised above the trout, the hand with the frying-pan was thrust under it. The scissors cut the line, the trout fell into the pan; hands, scissors and pan withdrew, the blind closed: all in the space of a second. Marcovaldo was totally bewildered.

"Are you also a cat-lover?" A voice at his back made him turn round. He was surrounded by little old women, some of them ancient, wearing old-fashioned hats on their heads; others, younger, but with the look of spinsters; and all were carrying in their hands or their bags packages of leftover meat or fish, and some even had little pans of milk. "Will you help me throw this package over the fence, for those poor creatures?"

All the ladies, cat-lovers, gathered at this hour around the garden of dry leaves to take food to their protégés.

"Can you tell me why they are all here, these cats?" Marcovaldo inquired.

"Where else could they go? This garden is all they have left! Cats come here from other neighborhoods, too, from miles and miles around . . ."

"And birds, as well," another lady added. "They're forced to live by the hundreds and hundreds on these few trees . . ."

"And the frogs, they're all in that pool, and at night they never stop croaking . . . You can hear them even on the eighth floor of the buildings around here."

"Who does this villa belong to anyway?" Marcovaldo asked. Now, outside the gate, there weren't just the cat-loving ladies but also other people: the man from the gas pump opposite, the apprentices from a mechanic's shop, the postman, the grocer, some passers-by. And none of them, men and women, had to be asked twice: all wanted to have their say, as always when a mysterious and controversial subject comes up.

"It belongs to a Marchesa. She lives there, but you never see her . . ."

"She's been offered millions and millions, by developers, for this little patch of land, but she won't sell . . ."

"What would she do with millions, an old woman all alone in the world? She wants to hold on to her house, even if it's falling to pieces, rather than be forced to move . . ."

"It's the only undeveloped bit of land in the downtown area . . . Its value goes up every year . . . They've made her offers –"

"Offers! That's not all. Threats, intimidation, persecution . . . You don't know the half of it! Those contractors!"

"But she holds out. She's held out for years . . ."

"She's a saint. Without her, where would those poor animals go?"

"A lot she cares about the animals, the old miser! Have you ever seen her give them anything to eat?"

"How can she feed the cats when she doesn't have food for herself? She's the last descendant of a ruined family!"

"She hates cats. I've seen her chasing them and hitting them with an umbrella!"

"Because they were tearing up her flowerbeds!"

"What flower-beds? I've never seen anything in this garden but a great crop of weeds!"

Marcovaldo realized that with regard to the old Marchesa opinions were sharply divided: some saw her as an angelic being, others as an egoist and a miser.

"It's the same with the birds; she never gives them a crumb!"

"She gives them hospitality. Isn't that plenty?"

"Like she gives the mosquitoes, you mean. They all come from here, from that pool. In the summertime the mosquitoes eat us alive, and it's all the fault of that Marchesa!"

"And the mice? This villa is a mine of mice. Under the dead leaves they have their burrows, and at night they come out . . ."

"As far as the mice go, the cats take care of them . . ."

"Oh, you and your cats! If we had to rely on them . . ."

"Why? Have you got something to say against cats?"

Here the discussion degenerated into a general quarrel.

"The authorities should do something: confiscate the villa!" one man cried.

"What gives them the right?" another protested.

"In a modern neighborhood like ours, a mouse-nest like this . . . it should be forbidden . . ."

"Why, I picked my apartment precisely because it overlooked this little bit of green . . ."

"Green, hell! Think of the fine skyscraper they could build here!"

Marcovaldo would have liked to add something of his own, but he couldn't get a word in. Finally, all in one breath, he exclaimed: "The Marchesa stole a trout from me!"

The unexpected news supplied fresh ammunition to the old woman's enemies, but her defenders exploited it as proof of the indigence to which the unfortunate noblewoman was reduced. Both sides agreed that Marcovaldo should go and knock at her door to demand an explanation.

It wasn't clear whether the gate was locked or unlocked; in any case, it opened, after a push, with a mournful creak. Marcovaldo picked his way among the leaves and cats, climbed the steps to the porch, knocked hard at the entrance.

At a window (the very one where the frying-pan had appeared), the blind was raised slightly and in one corner a round, pale blue eye was seen, and a clump of hair dyed an undefinable color, and a dry skinny hand. A voice was heard, asking: "Who is it? Who's at the door?", the words accompanied by a cloud smelling of fried oil.

"It's me, Marchesa. The trout man," Marcovaldo explained. "I don't mean to trouble you. I only wanted to tell you, in case you didn't know, that the trout was stolen from me, by that cat, and I'm the one who caught it. In fact the line . . ."

"Those cats! It's always those cats . . ." the Marchesa said, from behind the shutter, with a shrill, somewhat nasal voice. "All my troubles come from the cats! Nobody knows what I go through! Prisoner night and day of those horrid beasts! And with all the refuse people throw over the walls, to spite me!"

"But my trout . . ."

"Your trout! What am I supposed to know about your trout!" The Marchesa's voice became almost a scream, as if she wanted to drown out the sizzle of the oil in the pan, which came through the window along with the aroma of fried fish. "How can I make sense of anything, with all the stuff that rains into my house?"

"I understand, but did you take the trout or didn't you?"

"When I think of all the damage I suffer because of the cats! Ah, fine state of affairs! I'm not responsible for anything! I can't tell you what I've lost! Thanks to those cats, who've occupied house and garden for years! My life at the mercy of those animals! Go and find the owners! Make them pay damages! Damages? A whole life destroyed! A prisoner here, unable to move a step!"

"Excuse me for asking: but who's forcing you to stay?"

From the crack in the blind there appeared sometimes a round, pale blue eye, sometimes a mouth with two protruding teeth; for a moment the whole face was visible, and to Marcovaldo it seemed, bewilderingly, the face of a cat.

"They keep me prisoner, they do, those cats! Oh, I'd be glad to leave! What wouldn't I give for a little apartment all my own, in a nice clean modern building! But I can't go out . . . They follow me, they block my path, they trip me up!" The voice became a whisper, as if to confide a secret. "They're afraid I'll sell the lot . . . They won't leave me . . . won't allow me . . . When the builders come to offer me a contract, you should see them, those cats! They get in the way, pull out their claws; they even chased a lawyer off! Once I had the contract right here, I was about to sign it, and they dived in through the window, knocked over the inkwell, tore up all the pages . . ."

All of a sudden Marcovaldo remembered the time, the shipping department, the boss. He tiptoed off over the dried leaves, as the voice continued to come through the slats of the blind, enfolded in that cloud apparently from the oil of a frying-pan. "They even scratched me . . . I still have the scar . . . All alone here at the mercy of these demons . . ."

Winter came. A blossoming of white flakes decked the branches and capitals and the cats' tails. Under the snow, the dry leaves dissolved into mush. The cats were rarely seen, the cat-lovers even less; the packages of fish-bones were consigned only to cats who came to the door. Nobody, for quite a while, had seen anything of the Marchesa. No smoke came now from the chimneypot of the villa.

One snowy day, the garden was again full of cats, who had returned as if it were spring, and they were miauing as if on a moonlight night. The neighbors realized that something had happened: they went and knocked at the Marchesa's door. She didn't answer: she was dead.

In the spring, instead of the garden, there was a huge building site that a contractor had set up. The steam shovels dug down to great depths to make room for the foundations, cement poured into the iron armatures, a very high crane passed beams to the workmen who were making the scaffoldings. But how could they get on with their work? Cats walked along all the planks, they made bricks fall and upset buckets of mortar, they fought in the midst of the piles of sand. When you started to raise an armature, you found a cat perched on the top of it, hissing fiercely. More treacherous pusses climbed onto the masons' backs as if to purr, and there was no getting rid of them. And the birds continued making their nests in all the trestles, the cab of the crane looked like an aviary . . . And you couldn't dip up a bucket of water that wasn't full of frogs, croaking and hopping . . .

WINTER

20. Santa's Children

No period of the year is more gentle and good, for the world of industry and commerce, than Christmas and the weeks preceding it. From the streets rises the tremulous sound of the mountaineers' bagpipes; and the big companies, till yesterday coldly concerned with calculating gross product and dividends, open their hearts to human affections and to smiles. The sole thought of Boards of Directors now is to give joy to their fellow-man, sending gifts accompanied by messages of goodwill both to other companies and to private individuals; every firm feels obliged to buy a great stock of products from a second firm to serve as presents to third firms; and those firms, for their part, buy from yet another firm further stocks of presents for the others; the office windows remain aglow till late, specially those of the shipping department, where the personnel work overtime wrapping packages and boxes; beyond the misted panes, on the sidewalks covered by a crust of ice, the pipers advance. Having descended from the dark mysterious mountains, they stand at the downtown intersections, a bit dazzled by the excessive lights, by the excessively rich shop-windows; and heads bowed, they blow into their instruments; at that sound among the businessmen the heavy conflicts of interest are placated and give way to a new rivalry: to see who can

112

present the most conspicuous and original gift in the most attractive way.

At Sbav and Co. that year the Public Relations Office suggested that the Christmas presents for the most important persons should be delivered at home by a man dressed as Santa Claus.

The idea won the unanimous approval of the top executives. A complete Santa Claus outfit was bought: white beard, red cap and tunic edged in white fur, big boots. They had the various delivery men try it on, to see whom it fitted best, but one man was too short and the beard touched the ground; another was too stout and couldn't get into the tunic; another was too young; yet another was too old and it wasn't worth wasting make-up on him.

While the head of the Personnel Office was sending for other possible Santas from the various departments, the assembled executives sought to develop the idea: the Human Relations Office wanted the employees' Christmas packages also to be distributed by Santa Claus, at a collective ceremony; the Sales Office wanted Santa to make a round of the shops as well; the Advertising Office was worried about the prominence of the firm's name, suggesting that perhaps they should tie four balloons to a string with the letters S.B.A.V.

All were caught up in the lively and cordial atmosphere spreading through the festive, productive city; nothing is more beautiful than the sensation of material goods flowing on all sides and, with it, the good will each feels towards the others; for this, this above all, as the skirling sound of the pipes reminds us, is what really counts.

In the shipping department, goods – material and spiritual – passed through Marcovaldo's hands, since it represented merchandise to load and unload. And it was not only through loading and unloading that he shared in the general festivity, but also by thinking that at the end of that labyrinth of hundreds of thousands of packages there waited a package belonging to him alone, prepared by the Human Relations

Office; and even more, by figuring how much was due
him at the end of the month, counting the Christmas
bonus and his overtime hours. With that money, he too
would be able to rush to the shops and buy, buy, buy,
to give presents, presents, presents, as his most sincere
feelings and the general interests of industry and commerce
decreed.

The head of the Personnel Office came into the shipping
department with a fake beard in his hand. "Hey, you!" he
said to Marcovaldo. "See how this beard looks on you.
Perfect! You're Santa then. Come upstairs. Get moving.
You'll be given a special bonus if you make fifty home
deliveries per day."

Got up as Santa Claus, Marcovaldo rode through the
city, on the saddle of the motorbike-truck laden with
packages wrapped in vari-colored paper, tied with pretty
ribbons, and decorated with twigs of mistletoe and holly.
The white cotton beard tickled him a little but it protected
his throat from the cold air.

His first trip was to his own home, because he couldn't
resist the temptation of giving his children a surprise. At
first, he thought, they won't recognize me. Then I bet
they'll laugh!

The children were playing on the stairs. They barely
looked up. "Hi, Papà."

Marcovaldo was let down. "Hmph . . . Don't you see
how I'm dressed?"

"How are you supposed to be dressed?" Pietruccio said.
"Like Santa Claus, right?"

"And you recognized me first thing?"

"Easy! We recognized Signor Sigismondo, too; and he
was disguised better than you!"

"And the janitor's brother-in-law!"

"And the father of the twins across the street!"

"And the uncle of Ernestina — the girl with the
braids!"

"All dressed like Santa Claus?" Marcovaldo asked, and

the disappointment in his voice wasn't due only to the failure of the family surprise, but also because he felt that the company's prestige had somehow been impaired.

"Of course. Just like you," the children answered. "Like Santa Claus. With a fake beard, as usual." And turning their backs on him, the children became absorbed again in their games.

It so happened that the Public Relations Offices of many firms had had the same idea at the same time; and they had recruited a great number of people, jobless for the most part, pensioners, street-vendors, and had dressed them in the red tunic, with the cotton-wool beard. The children, the first few times, had been amused, recognizing acquaintances under that disguise, neighborhood figures, but after a while they were jaded and paid no further attention.

The game they were involved in seemed to absorb them entirely. They had gathered on a landing and were seated in a circle. "May I ask what you're plotting?" Marcovaldo inquired.

"Leave us alone, Papà; we have to fix our presents."

"Presents for who?"

"For a poor child. We have to find a poor child and give him presents."

"Who said so?"

"It's in our school reader."

Marcovaldo was about to say: "You're poor children yourselves!" But during this past week he had become so convinced that he was an inhabitant of the Land of Plenty, where all purchased and enjoyed themselves and exchanged presents, that it seemed bad manners to mention poverty; and he preferred to declare: "Poor children don't exist any more!"

Michelino stood up and asked: "Is that why you don't bring us presents, Papà?"

Marcovaldo felt a pang at his heart. "I have to earn some overtime now," he said hastily, "and then I'll bring you some."

"How do you earn it?"

"Delivering presents," Marcovaldo said.

"To us?"

"No, to other people."

"Why not to us? It'd be quicker."

Marcovaldo tried to explain. "Because I'm not the Human Relations Santa Claus, after all; I'm the Public Relations Santa Claus. You understand?"

"No."

"Never mind." But since he wanted somehow to apologize for coming home empty-handed, he thought he might take Michelino with him, on his round of deliveries. "If you're good, you can come and watch your Papà taking presents to people," he said, straddling the seat of the little delivery wagon.

"Let's go. Maybe I'll find a poor child," Michelino said and jumped on, clinging to his father's shoulders.

In the streets of the city Marcovaldo encountered only other red-and-white Santas, absolutely identical with him, who were driving panel-trucks or delivery carts or opening the doors of shops for customers laden with packages or helping carry their purchases to the car. And all these Santas seemed concentrated, busy, as if they were responsible for the operation of the enormous machine of the Holiday Season.

And exactly like them, Marcovaldo ran from one address to another, following his list, dismounted from his seat, sorted the packages in the wagon, selected one, presented it to the person opening the door, pronouncing the words: "Sbav and Company wish a Merry Christmas and a Happy New Year", and pocketed the tip.

This tip could be substantial and Marcovaldo might have been considered content, but something was missing. Every time, before ringing at a door, followed by Michelino, he anticipated the wonder of the person who, on opening the door, would see Santa Claus himself standing there before him; he expected some fuss, curiosity, gratitude. And every time he was received like the postman, who brings the newspaper day after day.

He rang at the door of a luxurious house. A governess answered the door. "Oh, another package. Who's this one from?"

"Sbav and Company wish a . . ."

"Well, bring it in," and she led Santa Claus down a corridor filled with tapestries, carpets, and majolica vases. Michelino, all eyes, followed his father.

The governess opened a glass door. They entered a room with a high ceiling, so high that a great fir tree could fit beneath it. It was a Christmas tree lighted by glass bubbles of every color, and from its branches hung presents and sweets of every description. From the ceiling hung heavy crystal chandeliers, and the highest branches of the fir caught some of the glistening drops. Over a large table were arrayed glass, silver, boxes of candied fruit and cases of bottles. The toys, scattered over a great rug, were as numerous as in a toyshop, mostly complicated electronic devices and model space-ships. On that rug, in an empty corner, there was a little boy about nine years old, lying prone, with a bored, sullen look. He was leafing through an illustrated volume, as if everything around him were no concern of his.

"Gianfranco, look. Gianfranco," the governess said. "You see? Santa Claus has come back with another present?"

"Three hundred twelve," the child sighed, without looking up from his book. "Put it over there."

"It's the three hundred and twelfth present that's arrived," the governess said. "Gianfranco is so clever. He keeps count; he doesn't miss one. Counting is his great passion."

On tiptoe Marcovaldo and Michelino left the house.

"Papà is that little boy a poor child?" Michelino asked.

Marcovaldo was busy rearranging the contents of the truck and didn't answer immediately. But after a moment, he hastened to protest: "Poor? What are you talking about?

You know who his father is? He's the president of the Society for the Implementation of Christmas Consumption. Commendatore –"

He broke off, because he didn't see Michelino anywhere. "Michelino! Michelino! Where are you?" He had vanished.

I bet he saw another Santa Claus go by, took him for me, and has gone off after him . . . Marcovaldo continued his rounds, but he was a bit concerned, and couldn't wait to get home again.

At home, he found Michelino with his brothers, good as gold.

"Say, where did you go?"

"I came home, to collect our presents . . . the presents for that poor child . . ."

"What? Who?"

"The one that was so sad . . . the one in the villa, with the Christmas tree . . ."

"Him? What kind of a present could you give him?"

"Oh, we fixed them up very nice . . . three presents, all wrapped in silver paper."

The younger boys spoke up: "We all went together to take them to him! You should have seen how happy he was!"

"I'll bet!" Marcovaldo said. "That was just what he needed to make him happy: your presents!"

"Yes, ours! . . . He ran over right away to tear off the paper and see what they were . . ."

"And what were they?"

"The first was a hammer: that big round hammer, the wooden kind . . ."

"What did he do then?"

"He was jumping with joy! He grabbed it and began to use it!"

"How?"

"He broke all the toys! And all the glassware! Then he took the second present . . ."

"What was that?"

"A slingshot. You should of seen him. He was so happy! He hit all the glass balls on the Christmas tree. Then he started on the chandeliers . . ."

"That's enough. I don't want to hear any more! And the . . . third present?"

"We didn't have anything left to give, so we took some silver paper and wrapped up a box of kitchen matches. That was the present that made him happiest of all. He said: They never let me touch matches! He began to strike them, and . . ."

"And?"

". . . and he set fire to everything!"

Marcovaldo was tearing his hair. "I'm ruined!"

The next day, turning up at work, he felt the storm brewing. He dressed again as Santa Claus, in great haste, loaded the presents to be delivered onto the truck, already amazed that no one had said anything to him, and then he saw, coming towards him, the three section chiefs: the one from Public Relations, the one from Advertising, and the one from Sales.

"Stop!" they said to him. "Unload everything. At once!"

This is it, Marcovaldo said to himself, and could already picture himself fired.

"Hurry up! We have to change all the packages!" the three section chiefs said. "The Society for the Implementation of Christmas Consumption has launched a campaign to push the Destructive Gift!"

"On the spur of the moment like this," one of the men remarked. "They might have thought of it sooner . . ."

"It was a sudden inspiration the President had," another chief explained. "It seems his little boy was given some ultra-modern gift-articles, Japanese, I believe, and for the first time the child was obviously enjoying himself . . ."

"The important thing," the third added, "is that the Destructive Gift serves to destroy articles of every sort: just what's needed to speed up the pace of consumption and give the market a boost . . . All in minimum time and within a child's capacities . . . The President of the Society sees a whole new horizon opening out. He's in seventh heaven, he's so enthusiastic . . ."

"But this child . . ." Marcovaldo asked, in a faint voice: "did he really destroy much stuff?"

"It's hard to make an estimate, even a hazy one, because the house was burned down . . ."

Marcovaldo went back to the street, illuminated as if it were night, crowded with Mammas and children and uncles and grannies and packages and balloons and rocking horses and Christmas trees and Santa Clauses and chickens and turkeys and fruit cakes and bottles and bagpipers and chimney-sweeps and chestnut vendors shaking pans of chestnuts over round, glowing, black stoves.

And the city seemed smaller, collected in a luminous vessel, buried in the dark heart of a forest, among the age-old trunks of the chestnut trees and an endless cloak of snow. Somewhere in the darkness the howl of the wolf was heard; the hares had a hole buried in the snow, in the warm red earth under a layer of chestnut burrs.

A jack-hare came out, white, onto the snow, he twitched his ears, ran beneath the moon, but he was white and couldn't be seen, as if he weren't there. Only his little paws left a light print on the snow, like little clover leaves. Nor could the wolf be seen, for he was black and stayed in the black darkness of the forest. Only if he opened his mouth, his teeth were visible, white and sharp.

There was a line where the forest, all black, ended and the snow began, all white. The hare ran on this side, and the wolf on that.

The wolf saw the hare's prints on the snow and followed them, always keeping in the black, so as not to be seen. At the point where the prints ended there should be the hare, and the wolf came out of the black, opened wide his red maw and his sharp teeth, and bit the wind.

The hare was a bit farther on, invisible; he scratched one ear with his paw, and escaped, hopping away.

Is he here? There? Is he a bit farther on?

Only the expanse of snow could be seen, white as this page.